The Troubling Adventures of
Jesse and Owen

by Ted Lemon

RoseDog Books
PITTSBURGH, PENNSYLVANIA 15238

RoseDog Books
585 Alpha Drive
Pittsburgh, PA 15238
Visit our website at *www.rosedogbookstore.com*

ISBN: 978-1-4809-7153-0
eISBN: 978-1-4809-7130-1

Chapter One

The sun shone brightly down on Jesse as he stood in the wooded area next to the railroad tracks. The warm wind blew his dark hair and made it stand straight up. It reminded him that he really needed a haircut. His hair was *always* scruffy, but it had gotten really long and his mother had been pestering him to get it cut for over a week now. He couldn't help but think that, if he held out just a little longer, she'd finally cave and let him get the Mohawk he'd wanted.

He chuckled to himself. He knew that even if she didn't cave, he'd just cut it himself.

Jesse was eight years old but, despite being young, had lived a great deal of life already. To Jesse, each day was an adventure waiting to happen, and now that third grade had ended and summer vacation had started, he had plenty of time for adventures.

The weather had been beautiful during the week since school had let out, but Jesse was already starting to get bored. He'd made a list of things he hoped to do this summer, and the list was almost finished already. He was gonna have to think of more stuff to do to keep himself busy. After all, the trailer park in which he lived was a big place with lots of fun to be had...one way or another.

There wasn't always someone to have fun with, but that was hardly his fault. There were plenty of other kids in the trailer park, but most were either too lame to keep up with Jesse or had been banned from hanging out with him by their parents. He'd even had a best friend for a while, Chris. They'd been very close until a little over a year ago when Chris's mother had decided that he was no longer allowed to hang out with Jesse.

1

Jesse had been upset at first, but he'd grown to accept it. He even started to like having his adventures on his own. Having no one to answer to was kinda nice. Who needed friends anyway? Not Jesse.

The sound of the train whistle in the distance snapped him back to the here and now. The train was almost here, and if he didn't hurry, he'd miss his chance.

He ran forward and quickly placed a toy action figure on the train track. It fell off. He placed it back on, waited to make sure that it would stay and then ran back to the safety of the trees. He quickly turned, covered his ears, and looked on with anticipation. *It HAD to work this time*, Jesse thought.

This was his third attempt at getting the train to smash his toy. Each time, the action figure fell off of the track before the train could hit it, and Jesse was getting more and more frustrated. The whistle blew again as the train rumbled closer. Jesse watched the action figure start to vibrate slowly as the train approached. He held his breath. *Just a few seconds more*, he thought.

A split second before the train would have hit it, the vibration made the toy bounce off of the track. Frustrated once again, Jesse lowered his head and let out a curse that was drowned out by the commotion of the train as it passed.

Once the train was gone, Jesse crept from his hiding spot and retrieved the action figure. He stared at it in disgust. "Guess I'm gonna have to find something else to do with you," Jesse said to the figure. Its neutral face stared mockingly back at him.

Just then he heard his mom calling him. Must be time for her to go to work. He shoved the toy into his pocket and began walking home. He wove a path through the trees to the field that was behind the trailer park and found the path that led home.

As he approached his home, he noticed some men working on the roof of a trailer a few down from his. They must have been finishing for the day because they were putting a tarp over buckets of roofing tar and their equipment.

As Jesse walked through the door, his mom was putting TV dinners in the oven. She wore light blue scrubs because she worked midnights as a nurse's aide at a local urgent care facility. She was tall, thin and was, Jesse guessed, reasonably attractive. She was in her late thirties but looked slightly older with long brown hair that had some grey throughout. The grey was in no doubt partly due to the stress of raising Jesse and his older brother, Jacob, on her own.

She saw him come in the door and smiled. "I'm getting ready to leave, Jess, but dinner is in the oven," she said as she walked to the bathroom.

Jesse followed her past the couch, where he noticed his brother, Jacob, sitting. Jacob gave him a sly smile as he passed. Jesse knew full well what was coming next. He leaned against the door jamb of the bathroom as his mother fixed her hair. "Jesse, your brother is in charge," she said firmly, obviously ready for the argument that she was sure to come.

Despite her firm tone, Jesse began what had become the same old speech, "But *Mom*, Jacob treats me like crap!" He continued, "As soon as you leave, his friends come over and they all gang up on me!"

Jacob overheard their conversation as he walked out of his bedroom and yelled, "Quit whining, you little turd." Without missing a beat, Jesse pointed at his brother and said loudly, "See?"

He'd never been close to his older brother. It used to bother Jesse when he was younger. All he'd ever wanted was for Jacob to show some interest in him. Show that he liked having a little brother but Jacob had always bullied him and treated Jesse like a nuisance. Now that Jesse was getting older, it was getting harder for him to just sit back and take it.

"Cut it out," Jesse's mom said as she walked to the living room, with Jesse still following, "Both of you!"

She took a deep, calming breath and continued, "Listen, you know I need this job so you two had better learn to get along.

She grabbed her purse, kissed them both and whispered "Be nice" to Jacob as she wiped her lipstick off of his cheek with her thumb.

She blew them another kiss on her way out the door. The brothers smiled at her then looked at each other in disgust but said nothing.

Jesse went to the oven to get his TV dinner, grabbed some silverware and sat on the couch. He turned the TV on as Jacob made a phone call. About five minutes later, Jacob hung up the phone and said, 'Curtis and Tommy will be here soon so don't even think of giving me any crap!'" Suddenly, Jesse no longer had an appetite.

Jacob's friends and teammates on the JV football team, Curtis and Tommy, arrived a little while later. While not quite as big as Jacob, both of them were still much bigger than Jesse. They immediately took the TV remote from Jesse. "C'mon!" Jesse yelled as he stood up to confront the older boys.

Jesse only came up to Curtis's shoulders but that wasn't about to stop him. Furious, he puffed his chest out and bumped the older boy. Curtis, momentarily surprised, took a step back. "Oh, look at the BIG MAN!" he said as he stepped toward Jesse.

Curtis put Jesse in a headlock. "Come on big man, say it!" Curtis growled. "Let me go!" Jesse responded. "Not until you SAY IT!" Curtis said, this time a little more forcefully. After a few seconds, Jesse reluctantly swallowed his pride enough to say "Curtis rules!'

Curtis let Jesse go, lightly patted Jesse's face and said "Good BOY." Jesse straightened his hair and scowled at Curtis.

Jacob stepped between Curtis and Jesse and said, "Beat it, turd."
Jesse opened his mouth to argue but thought better of it and just sulked to his room.

As he was closing his bedroom door, he had an idea and the scowl that had been on his face turned into an evil smile.

An hour later, Jacob heard a loud thud come from Jesse's room. He went to investigate.

When he reached Jesse's room, he knocked on the door and said, "You better not be breaking stuff in there."

No answer. He knocked again. Still no answer so he slowly opened the door and looked inside.

The window was open, but no one was in the room. Jacob crossed the room to the window and looked outside. He expected to see his brother outside, hiding or something, but no one was there.

It had started to get dark outside, but just as he was getting ready to close the window, he noticed something in the grass. He stopped and poked his head out to get a better look. There, on the grass, were three pairs of shoes. *Their* shoes!

Jacob, in a fit of rage, climbed out of the window and jumped down onto the grass, but as soon as his socked feet touched the ground he realized something was wrong.

The grass was slimy, and sticky. He tried to move but found he couldn't. His feet were stuck to the grass by some thick goo.

Jacob leaned toward the window and called for Curtis and Tommy. After a few seconds, the boys came into Jesse's bedroom and looked out of the window.

"I'm stuck, guys," Jacob angrily said, "go around the front and come pull me out!" Tommy and Curtis looked at Jacob's feet and saw that he was, indeed, stuck. Then they looked at each other and began to laugh hysterically.

The boys laughed until they saw the shoes. Once the laughter had died off and they realized just what was going on, they followed Jacob's instructions and went through the house, out the front door and around the trailer to where Jacob waited.

It took a few tries, but his friends managed to pull Jacob free of the sludge but before they could get their shoes, Jesse came to the window, smiling mischievously.

Jesse closed and locked the window. Jacob met Jesse's eyes and scowled. The brothers stared at each other for what seemed like an hour, neither one blinking. Without taking his eyes off of Jesse, Jacob said, "Quick, back to the front!"

The three older boys ran around the trailer, in their socks, to the front door and found it locked as well. Jacob pounded his fist on the door and cursed. Then he had an idea. "C'mon," he said.

Jacob, with his friends following, made his way back around the trailer, but this time to his own bedroom window, and found it slightly ajar. Jacob smiled as he thought of all the horrible things he was going to do to his brother.

As Jacob was trying to lift the window the rest of the way open, the bedroom light suddenly popped on. Jesse was standing in the room with a rope in his hands.

Jacob followed the rope with his eyes. It crossed the room, went out the window and then up. He hadn't even noticed it until now. Jesse smiled again and pulled the rope. Jacob and his friends looked up just as a bucket of roofing tar dumped onto them.

The next day, Jesse was outside scrubbing remnants of the roofing tar off of the front porch and walkway. It was his punishment for the chaos he'd created the previous night.

After the incident with the tar, Jesse had barricaded himself in his bedroom until his mother returned from work.

As mad as Jacob was, his mother was even angrier, and worse, she didn't care that Jacob's friends had started the whole thing. She had grounded Jesse until the mess was cleaned up.

He scrubbed for a while and then decided to take a break. After all, no one was watching him. His mom was sleeping after working most of the night and Jacob was gone. Jacob had been encouraged by his mother to sleep at Curtis's house, mainly so she didn't have to worry about him killing Jesse while she slept.

The three older boys had mostly ignored Jesse while they washed as much as the tar off of themselves as they could. They'd shot Jesse the occasional dirty look, but that was it.

Jesse went inside, got himself a can of pop, and then went outside to relax. It was a beautiful day, and he couldn't stand the thought of wasting it scrubbing tar.

He was sitting in the grass in front of his house when a yellow Monte Carlo pulled onto his street. Jesse didn't know much about cars, but he could tell that this car was cool. It wasn't new or anything, but it was obviously well taken care of.

The car stopped in front of a trailer two spots down from Jesse's, and a man exited from the driver's side. The man stretched and then started to walk around the front of the car but stopped short as he noticed something. He leaned over the hood of the car and wiped off a smudge.

Apparently satisfied that his car was back in acceptable condition, he continued around to the other side of the car where a woman had exited from the passenger seat.

The man and woman stood staring at the empty trailer for a few seconds, then went to the trunk of the car. They began removing boxes and walking with them towards the trailer. The woman was almost to the door when she turned and yelled back toward the car, "You coming?'

The rear passenger door opened, and a young boy stepped out. He was thin, had a very pallid complexion, wore a lime green t-shirt, brown shorts, and glasses that were almost as big as his face. His sandy blonde hair was parted down the middle and stayed firm despite the slight breeze. Jesse guessed that the boy was maybe a little taller than he was but looked like they'd be close in age.

The boy looked around, used his index finger to push his glasses up further on his nose, and then reached into the backseat of the Monte Carlo. He pulled out a small box, turned, and started to walk toward the trailer.

"Hey!" Jesse called out. The other boy stopped and looked around again, startled, until he saw Jesse.

"Me?" the boy asked.

Jesse ignored the question. "You moving in?" he asked.

"Um, yeah." the boy replied.

"What's your name?" Jesse asked, determined to get as much info as possible on this new kid.

The boy pushed his glasses up with his finger again, looked down at his box, and then quietly said, "Owen."

Chapter Two

The next day, Owen was eating a bowl of cereal at the kitchen table in his new home as his mom tackled the tedious job of unpacking.

"So, where's Tom?" Owen asked his mom. Tom was technically his stepfather but Owen refused to call him that. He was married to Owen's mom but, to him, that didn't make Tom his stepfather.

Owen's mom kept unpacking but said, "Out trying to find a job." Owen just stared at her. She didn't notice at first but eventually his silence made her turn to look at him. She acknowledged the skeptical look on his face with a sigh and said, "Okay, looking for a job AND getting his car washed," she said.

Satisfied, Owen went back to his breakfast. He knew that most guys loved their cars, but Tom loved *his* car more than anything. Owen wouldn't be surprised if Tom spent the whole day fixing up his car and not looking for a job at all.

In between bites of cereal, Owen heard a small popping sound coming from outside. Curious, he quickly finished his breakfast and asked his mom if he could go outside to explore. She told him to stay close until he found his way around.

Owen stepped outside and blinked the harsh sunlight away. He'd never been much of an outdoorsy type, and the bright sunlight felt like something he'd never get used to.

It *was* a nice day though, if you were into that sort of thing, and by the looks of the activity around the trailer park, many kids *were* into that sort of thing.

Everywhere he looked, there was something going on. Kids were riding bikes in the street, a group of girls were playing a game. Foursquare, Owen thought it was called. He saw a bunch of older boys playing basketball over by the park office.

Then he saw the boy sitting by himself on the sidewalk a few trailers down. It was the same boy from yesterday, Jesse.

Owen stood and stared at Jesse for a few minutes. He watched as Jesse repeatedly used a rock to hit something on the sidewalk. After a few hits, a loud pop occurred and Jesse laughed.

Owen wasn't sure if he should go talk to Jesse. After all, it had been kind of weird how Jesse had just started talking to him the way he did. Then again, Owen wasn't entirely sure if Jesse was the weird one or he himself.

After much deliberation, Owen decided to go see what Jesse was doing.

He walked shyly up to the sidewalk where Jesse was kneeling and stood there. Jesse looked up and said "Hey, what's up new kid?"

Nodding towards the red squares on the sidewalk, Owen said, "What are you doing?"

"Oh, I found these things in a box in my grandma's garage," Jesse said, holding up a roll of the red squares, "Look! They have real gunpowder in them!"

With a worried look forming on his face, Owen said "That sounds dangerous!"

"Nah," Jesse assured, "Here, lemme show ya." He spread the roll on the sidewalk and began hitting it with the rock. After a few misses, he made contact with the small circle in the middle that held the gunpowder. CRACK! It was much louder when you were up close.

"Here, you try," Jesse said. Owen was hesitant. He lowered his gaze to his hands and wrung them nervously. He looked over his shoulder toward his new home.

Despite his inner turmoil, he decided to give it a try. He knelt down and grabbed the rock. It took him just two tries before he hit the little red dot in the center. CRACK! With that loud crack, he felt a surge of excitement.

"See?" Jesse said. "You're a natural, kid."

They both continued popping the caps for the next hour and got to know each other.

Jesse told Owen how he lived with his mom and older brother, Jacob, and how they had moved here after his dad had left them when Jesse was just three years old. He told Owen about his mom's issues finding a steady job until finding this latest one working midnights.

Owen felt an instant kinship with Jesse. He also lived with his mother, but she was married to Owen's stepfather, Tom. Owen was an only child and had actually never met his real father because he had died before Owen was born.

That's all that Owen seemed willing to share so Jesse changed the subject.

"So dude," he said, "what do you like to do?"

Owen didn't hesitate, "I read a lot!"

Jesse rolled his eyes. "I mean what do you like to do for *fun?*"

Owen tilted his head slightly, pushed his glasses up and said, "Reading *is* fun."

"Yeah, maybe when you're old," Jesse half joked. "What *else* do you like to do," he asked.

Owen thought for a moment and said, "I like chemistry. My mom gave me a chemistry set for my birthday this year."

Jesse's eyes lit up. "*Now* we're talkin'!"

A few minutes later, Jesse crouched below Owen's window. The window opened and Owen's head popped out. "I can't find it," he said, "It's still packed."

"Just look some more," Jesse snapped at him. After another few minutes, Owen leaned out of the window and said, "Here," as he dropped a small box down to Jesse.

The window closed again, and a minute later Owen came running around the back of the trailer to where Jesse waited. "So what exactly do we need this stuff for," he asked.

"Come on and you'll see," Jesse said.

They ran with the box to the field behind the trailer park. Crouching in the grass on either side of the box, they opened it.

"So," Jesse said, looking incredibly excited, "what *is* all this stuff?"

Owen started listing off the chemicals.

Looking confused, Jesse said, "Yeah, that doesn't help." He looked inside the box once again and then back at Owen, "What do they *do?*'

"Well, they're all different', Owen began, "this is Potassium Hexacyanoferrate. It's used a lot for photography." Jesse nodded excitedly. "And this," Owen continued, "is Citric Acid. It's used fo–"

"Wait, hold up," Jesse interrupted quickly, "you've got ACID?"

"Yes," Owen said, a little hesitantly.

Jesse just stared blankly at the bottle, "like, *real* acid?"

Jesse's eyes went wide before Owen could answer, and a mischievous smile spread across his face as he quickly stood up and said, "I've got an idea, come on!"

Owen quickly gathered the contents of the box and followed Jesse.

They ran to Jesse's trailer. Owen waited outside with the box while Jesse went inside. Less than a minute later he came out carrying a backpack. "Come on," he said. Owen was getting a bad feeling about this.

The boys ran across the field to the wooded area. Just inside the trees, Jesse stopped by a large, flat rock. The rock had what looked like burnt marks all over it. It was mostly black on top, but it also had small splatters of another, multi-colored, substance. Wax? Plastic?

Jesse smiled proudly, "I call it my sacrifice stone." He nodded toward the rock as he knelt down and opened the backpack. Now was Owen's turn to look appalled. *Sacrifice stone?*

Jesse reached inside the backpack and pulled out an action figure. He placed it on the stone and said, "Lemme have that citris acid."

"Um, CITRIC acid," Owen corrected, handing him the bottle.

"Whatever," Jesse said as he gently opened the bottle and held it above the action figure, "ready?" His eyes flashed with evil delight.

"I guess so," Owen said warily.

Jesse slowly poured the acid on the miniature man and waited. He leaned forward intently. The toy changed color slightly but not much else happened.

"Um, Jesse," Owen began as he noticed the look of disappointment creeping onto Jesse's face, "citric acid isn't really that strong." Jesse's heart sank as he watched his action figure just laying there. At this rate, he thought to himself, it would be days before the toy dissolved entirely.

Jesse reached for the figure and pinched it by the foot, knowing that the acid hadn't hit there. He pulled, but the toy stuck to the rock slightly.

Just then, he heard the train whistle in the distance. His eyes went wide yet again as another idea popped into his head. Perhaps the plan could be salvaged after all.

He pulled a little harder and the figure peeled away from the rock. It was starting to soften, but it was still intact.

He ran to the tracks and gently placed the toy on the rail as Owen watched over his shoulder. Jesse picked up a small rock and used it to press the figure down on the track. It stuck!

The boys then ran back to the cover of the trees as the train rumbled closer. They covered their ears and watched the train pass, running over the action figure in the process.

After the train had passed, both boys went to see the damage and weren't disappointed. The action figure wasn't just smashed, it was obliterated. Most of it was flat, having been softened by the acid, but there were a few pieces lying next to the track.

Jesse was elated that his idea had finally come to fruition. "YES!" He said excitedly, "I finally got that thing to stay!"

"And I couldn't have done it without you," Jesse said. "I have a feeling," he continued, "that you and I are gonna be great friends!"

"Um, Jesse," Owen began, a little sheepishly, "why didn't you just use glue to make it stay?"

The boys walked home, having been called for dinner. As they walked, Jesse told Owen about Jacob and the incident with the tar. Normally, he wouldn't even think of sharing his problems with someone, but this kid was different. Plus, it felt kinda good to share...though he couldn't imagine making a habit of it.

The new friends waved goodbye as the sun was starting its slow descent in the sky. "See you tomorrow, dude?" Jesse asked.

"Yeah. Um, sure...dude," Owen said with a smile.

Jesse grinned and shook his head, "I've got *so* much to teach you."

Chapter Three

The next morning, Owen awoke in a great mood. How could he not? For the very first time, he had a friend. Someone who, while different than he was, seemed to accept Owen for who he is.

As he dressed, Owen thought about the fun that he'd had yesterday with Jesse. He couldn't recall having a better day with someone his own age.

"OWEN!" came a deep, booming voice. Owen's good mood came to a screeching halt. It was Tom, and if Tom was calling him, that meant that Owen's mom wasn't home, and that wasn't good. For Owen at least.

He knew from past experience that ignoring Tom's call would only make things worse so he crept timidly from his bedroom and down the hall that lead to the living room.

Tom was there, sitting in the usual place, his recliner. He had a lit cigarette in the corner of his mouth as he stared blankly at the TV. From the looks of it, he'd been up for a long time. Three empty beer cans sat next to him on the end table and the ashtray was filled with crushed out butts.

"Y-yes?" Owen said quietly.

"Make me a sandwich," Tom said, without even a glance in Owen's direction. He'd learned not to defy Tom so Owen made for the kitchen right away.

He made the sandwich, gave it to his stepfather, and left the trailer as quickly as he could without drawing any more attention from Tom.

Today, Owen had been lucky that Tom seemed to be in a good mood, or at least not in a *bad* mood, and that was good enough.

He was halfway to Jesse's house when his friend came out of the door. Jesse had a piece of toast in his mouth as he came running up to him, out of breath. Seeing the toast reminded Owen that, in his haste, he'd forgotten to eat.

"'Sup, dude?" Jesse said around the toast.

"Uh, nothing," Owen replied, deciding to keep his fear of Tom under wraps. He worried that his new friend would somehow be driven away if he knew how messed up Owen's family was.

"Why are you out of breath?" Owen asked, happy to change the subject.

Jesse rolled his eyes and said, "Jacob cornered me as I was leaving."

"Uh oh, what happened?" Owen asked hurriedly.

"It was weird," Jesse started, "he just backed me into a corner and stared at me."

"He didn't say anything?"

Jesse shook his head, "Nope. Just stared at me."

Owen whistled quietly, glad to be talking about something other than his own family. Jesse said, "It kinda freaked me out."

They were both silent for a minute, then Jesse said, "So, whatcha wanna do?" They were both thankful for the change in subject.

"What *is* there to do?" Owen responded. Jesse sat down on the curb and began tying his shoes, which he'd forgotten to do in his rush to get away from his brother.

"Hey, you got any money?" Jesse asked Owen, looking up from his shoe. Owen didn't even have to think about it, "Nope." He hardly ever had any money of his own. He had a little in a piggy bank, but he wasn't supposed to touch that. "Why?'

Jesse stood back up and said, "Well, if we had money, we could go see the Dub."

Confused, Owen shrugged his shoulders as he asked, "What's the Dub?"

"Not what, *WHO*." Jesse answered, remembering that his friend was new around here. "Dub is the guy you go see when you're looking for those hard to find items."

Owen shrugged again and said, "I'll have to remember that. What else is there?'

Jesse thought for a minute, looking around, and then a smile crept onto his face. Owen didn't like the look of that smile. It was, as he was finding out, a smile that meant trouble.

"Do you like snakes?" Jesse asked, still smiling.

Owen was mortified, "God, no!" he said instantly.

Jesse's troubling look just got more intense, "Good, me either. Let's go find some."

Jesse took them to the field behind the trailer park and tried to show Owen how to search for snakes. "Jesse," Owen began, "I-I really don't like snakes...at ALL!"

Jesse sighed and gave Owen a look of pity. "So, let's find one and show it who's boss." Jesse said adamantly as he began walking through the tall grass.

Owen walked in the opposite direction, only halfway looking for a snake and not really knowing what he'd do if he happened to find one. After a few minutes, Owen heard Jesse say, "Dude. Come here!"

Owen ran to where Jesse was standing with his eyes fixated on something in the grass.

As he approached, Owen could see what Jesse had found. Three paint cans. All three looked used and had their lids loosely fitted in place.

They crouched down to get a better look. Jesse picked up one of the cans and peeled the lid up to reveal the white paint still inside. The can was still half full.

"Now THIS," Jesse said with an even bigger smile, putting the lid back in place and setting the can down, "I can work with!"

Just then, Owen saw movement in the grass a few feet away. "Snake!!!" Jesse quickly stood and ran toward the snake, yelling, "Step on it! Step on it!"

For a split second, it crossed Owen's mind that stepping on the snake might not be the best way to catch a live snake. Especially if you wanted to *keep* it alive. He tried anyway but missed. Jesse had reached him by that time and lunged forward with his own foot, pinning the snake in place.

"Jeez," Jesse said to Owen, "you almost let it get away." He bent down and grabbed the garter snake behind the head. The snake writhed in the boy's grip. At least it seemed unhurt, Owen thought. Jesse brought the snake level with his face and said "oh, you're a good one. You'll do just fine."

Owen was confused. "But you said that you didn't like snakes," he said.

"I don't," Jesse said with a shrug as he walked towards the woods, "and this one is gonna find out just how much I hate snakes."

Owen was starting to get a bad feeling as he followed his friend.

The snake wrapped itself around Jesse's hand as he carried it into the woods and to his sacrifice stone. Owen was starting to see what Jesse had in mind, and he didn't like it one bit.

Owen finally realized what the marks on the stone were. This wasn't the first unlucky living thing to be brought to this place.

Owen suddenly felt sick to his stomach. It was true that he didn't like snakes but this, whatever it was that Jesse had in mind, was too much.

"So what are you going to do with it?" Owen asked him.

Jesse shrugged again and said, "Don't know yet. Any ideas?"

Owen sheepishly said, "Let it go?"

Jesse seemed genuinely surprised that Owen could even *think* such a thing. "Nah!" Jesse said, "What's the fun in that?"

Owen's mind raced. He tried thinking of something, *anything*, to take Jesse's focus from the sacrifice stone.

"Hey, I know," Owen blurted out, "why don't we scare someone with it?'

Jesse stopped to consider the thought and then smiled. Owen could actually see the beginning of another plan start to form in Jesse face. "You know," Jesse began, "we're not the only ones who don't like snakes."

Jesse began to lay out his devious plan for his friend. It was Saturday, and that meant that the ladies bingo club was going to be playing in the trailer park clubhouse.

"Oh boy," Owen said, looking worriedly at his friend. The bad feeling that had started to diminish was back with a vengeance.

"So you want to scare the old women at the clubhouse?" Owen asked, making sure that he'd heard Jesse right. Jesse smiled, "Bingo!" he said ironically.

A few minutes later, they were kneeling under a window of the clubhouse. Inside, they could hear the raucous sounds of a party. It sure didn't *sound* like bingo.

Jesse, still holding the snake, slowly peeked inside the window. He saw at least twenty women sitting at tables. They were playing bingo all right, but it was a lot rowdier than he'd imagined. All of the women were drinking frozen concoctions and seemed to be more concerned with the party than the game. It was the strangest sight he'd ever seen.

He lowered himself back down so he was level with Owen. "Looks like fun, I guess," Jesse said, "but it's missing something." He noticed Owen's confused look and lowered his own eyes to the snake, and smiled that evil smile.

"B-12," called the lady drawing the numbers. There came a loud response from the back of the room, "BINGO!" As the winner stood in excitement, there was a slight commotion from behind her. Then a scream, and then the room erupted into chaos.

Pretty soon it was complete chaos with women running everywhere and a lone garter snake slithering through the middle of the room.

Jesse was once again looking through the window, enjoying the chaos he'd created.

Owen peeked up also. As much as he'd like to deny it, it WAS pretty funny.

They watched the whole scene play out and then walked home, excitedly talking about how much fun it had been.

Chapter Four

The next day, Jesse awoke at his usual time, 7 A.M. He realized right away that it was gonna be a dreary day because the light coming through his window wasn't as bright as it should have been.

He sat up in his bed, looked out the window, saw rain, and sighed. There wasn't as much to do when you were stuck inside.

He got out of bed and walked to the bathroom, smelling bacon along the way. His spirits lightened knowing that his mom was making breakfast.

When he sat down at the table, his mother placed a plate with scrambled eggs and two pieces of bacon in front of him. She kissed his head and said, "good morning."

She sat across from him with her coffee. "Where's Jacob," Jesse asked. She gave him a knowing look and said, "Where do you think?" Still in bed, no doubt. He'd probably be there until noon, and Jesse was fine with that. He'd have some time to himself. Jacob had mostly gotten over the incident with the tar, but Jesse knew payback was gonna come eventually.

Jesse's mom headed off to bed for the day while he finished his breakfast.

He put his dishes in the sink, walked to the living room, and sat down on the couch. He glanced out of the window at the rain, coming down harder now. He grabbed the remote and turned the TV on. It was time for the best thing to do when you're stuck inside on a rainy day...play video games.

After an hour or so playing his favorite game, *Bug Annihilator*, he noticed the wind seemed to be picking up outside. Then suddenly, the power went out. "Aw, man!" Jesse said aloud.

There was enough light coming through the window for him to see but the problem was, with no power, there wasn't much TO see, and that meant one thing. That he was going to be bored.

An idea popped into his head. He got up and ran to his room. He quickly got dressed, put on a hoodie and a pair of boots, and then quietly went outside.

He splashed his way over to Owen's house, knocked on the door and waited, soaked from the rain.

A woman answered the door. She wore a light pink robe and looked as though she'd just gotten out of bed. "Is Owen home?" Jesse asked.

"Yes, he is," she said quickly as she opened the door and motioned for him to come inside.

Once inside, Jesse noticed the room was full of unpacked boxes. The living room, in which he stood, was mostly dark except for the light from a few candles that were burning.

The woman was staring at him, Jesse realized suddenly, no doubt wondering who this little wet kid was. She raised her eyebrows expectantly. "Oh, I'm Jesse," the wet boy offered as he stood there shivering.

The woman's eyes lit up. "OH! Owen has told me about you." she said excitedly. "Owen," the woman yelled over her shoulder, "Jesse is here to see you."

Owen came from the hallway and his eyes brightened, "Jesse!"

"Hey, dude," Jesse said, "can you hang out?"

"Well, Owen can't go outside in the rain, but you two can play in his room," the woman, said with a smile.

A few minutes later, the two boys were in Owen's bedroom. There was a small battery powered lantern on his dresser. Owen carried a flashlight as he was giving Jesse a formal tour.

Afterwards, Jesse couldn't hold his disbelief inside. "No video games?" he started. "Hardly any toys. Not even a TV!"

Jesse was just blown away. What WAS this kid? An alien!? All he had was science stuff.

Jesse could only hope that all the cool stuff was still packed, but Owen dashed those hopes pretty quickly. "This is the stuff I like to do," he said softly, sounding proud but somehow a little ashamed at the same time.

Jesse pointed at a full bookcase, "I mean, who reads THAT much?" Owen just shrugged. "Have you actually read all those?" Jesse asked.

"Yeah," Owen answered, "don't you like to read?"

"Me?" Jesse asked, sounding mortified at the thought. "NO!" He answered his own question.

Owen grabbed a book off of the shelf and sat down on his bed. "Don't you even realize that a book can take you *anywhere*?" Owen said, finally sounding confident about something. Passionate even. "With a book you can be anything," he continued, "be *anyone*! When I read a book, it takes me away from everything else I have going on. All of the bad stuff." Owen said, not meeting Jesse's gaze. "They let me have an adventure in my mind."

Jesse sat staring at Owen.

Owen decided to take a different approach. "You like video games right?" Owen asked.

Jesse gave a little snort and said, "Well, yeah. Who doesn't?"

Owen continued, "Okay, so what's your favorite game?"

Jesse answered quickly, not having to give it much thought, "Right now it's *Bug Annihilator*!"

Owen said, "Okay, well, what if you could do the same thing in your mind as you do in the game?"

Jesse still looked puzzled.

"Okay, let's try this," Owen said as he opened the book he'd retrieved. He turned to a section with purpose and then turned a few more pages. "Here we go," he said, "this story is about a group of explorers that get lost in a huge cave."

Jesse sat down next to Owen on the bed. Owen shifted the book onto both of their laps and shined the flashlight on it so they both could see. He read the first line of the story. "The deep chasm was a dream world of swirling colors as the last slivers of sunlight swam through the air and bounced from wall to jagged wall," Owen read, "Bright yellows, burning oranges and reds gave way to deep blues and velvety purple."

Owen turned the flashlight toward Jesse. Jesse gave a nod and a half smile.

"Okay, now close your eyes." Owen told him. Jesse did as he was told. Once satisfied that Jesse had his eyes closed, Owen read the last line again, slowly, "Bright yellows, burning oranges and reds gave way to deep blues and velvety purple."

As he finished, he turned the flashlight off and told Jesse to open his eyes...

...Jesse slowly opened his eyes to the most beautiful sight he'd ever seen. A huge cave sprawled out in front of him, stretching as far as his eyes could see. A million colors danced all around the cave.

Jesse, feeling something on his head, reached up to find a hard hat with a flashlight attached to the front. He looked down at himself and saw he was wearing climbing gear over his chest and around his waist.

Owen stood next to him in the middle of the cave wearing the same climbing gear. "Wow," Jesse exclaimed, "this is awesome!"

Owen smiled knowingly and said, "Well, don't just stand here. Let's go explore."

They began walking deeper into the cave. The sheer awesomeness of it left them speechless.

After a while, Jesse asked, "Is it always like this?"

"Depends." Owen replied. "It's whatever you want it to be."

Once again, Jesse noticed how Owen seemed different than the shy, uncomfortable kid he'd met just two days ago. THIS was his world. As they continued to walk, Jesse suddenly had a thought, "So…this can be whatever I want?"

"Yep," Owen replied.

Jesse stopped walking. At first Owen didn't notice but after a few steps, he stopped also.

He turned towards Jesse. "What are you—" he started but trailed off as he saw the look on Jesse's face.

Jesse was looking around at the walls of the cave again, but this time it was different. He was concentrating as he looked around, his head tilted slightly like he was listening for something.

Owen started to ask him what was going on when he heard something himself. It was a low rumble, seeming to come from everywhere. It was getting louder.

Jesse gave a quiet, "Shhhh…" as he slowly reached a hand around behind himself. His hand reappeared with some sort of futuristic looking gun.

Owen felt the quiet tranquil feeling he'd had quickly melting away. Jesse tentatively looked over at Owen and said, "We're not alone in here."
Owen swallowed hard.

"Grab your firearm soldier," Jesse ordered.

"What?" Owen asked.

"Do it," Jesse hissed, "NOW!"

Owen quickly fumbled behind his back, mostly for show, since he knew that there was nothing there. But there WAS something there. A holster held a gun similar to Jesse's.

He'd hardly had time to register the fact that he was now holding a gun when the first giant bug came burrowing through the cave wall to their right. Jesse turned a fired a yellowish green stream of liquid. The stuff glowed in the dark hissed as it cut the air towards the bug.

When the lava-like liquid hit the bug, it turned red. The bug exploded in a huge ball of green guts that splattered towards the boys. A glob of the disgusting stuff landed at Owen's feet. "Do NOT let that stuff get on you," Jesse screamed as he grabbed the collar of Owen's shirt, "you hear me soldier?" Owen nodded nervously. "You get any on ya and you'll turn into one of them," Jesse explained.

"Now, if you plan on living through this," Jesse continued, "you're gonna need to use that gun." Owen swallowed again, harder this time. Jesse leaned closer to Owen's face, "you with me soldier?'

Just then another bug, more of a slug this time, came shooting out of another hole in the wall. Owen pushed Jesse out of the way and shot it.

Breathing heavily from the excitement, the boys smiled at each other and then began annihilating some bugs.

There was a seemingly endless army of bugs coming out of various holes in the wall now. The boys relentlessly mowed them down with liquid death.

After the battle had concluded, they stood in the middle of the cave with bug carcasses surrounding them. They were both breathing heavily. Jesse put his hands on his knees and closed his eyes while trying to catch his breath.

He opened his eyes and noticed the spot of bug guts on Owen's leg. The putrid smelling mess had burned through the material of Owen's pants and was now eating into his skin.

"No," Jesse whispered. Owen followed his friends gaze and saw the bug guts on his skin. He realized that this was bad. Really bad.

Owen dropped to his knees as Jesse rushed forward to catch him. Owen was already showing signs of the turn. At this rate, Owen would be a bug in less than five minutes.

Jesse leaned Owen back and cradled his head. "Stay with me buddy," Jesse tried to console his friend. Owen's humanity was quickly slipping away and Jesse could do nothing to stop it.

He knew what he had to do. Slowly, silently, Jesse slipped his gun from its holster behind his back. He brought it up to Owen's head. "Don't worry soldier," Jesse said, choking back tears, "it'll be over soon."

The bedroom door opened, and Owen's mom peeked her head in. "Who wants a snack?" she asked.

The boys jumped up and said "ME!"

As Owen's mom left the room to get their snacks, both boys smiled at each other. "To be continued," Owen said.

Chapter Five

The month of June was rapidly coming to a close. It had already been almost two weeks since Jesse met his new friend Owen, and they were having many wonderful adventures together.

Jesse was even starting to like reading a little, but he found most of Owen's books kind of boring. Every time Owen showed him a new book, Jesse had to put his own spin on it to make it a little more fun.

Like their adventure in the cave, Jesse used his imagination to spice things up. So a trip to Africa for a safari became a life or death struggle with a pride of lions. An undersea dive became a treasure hunt that resulted in a battle with a great white shark...AND an octopus.

Owen had even let Jesse borrow a few books but again, they just couldn't capture his imagination enough. Combine that with the fact that he had to basically sneak the books in and out, it wasn't really worth it to borrow them. If Jacob found out that Jesse was spending his free time reading, Jesse knew that he'd be teased relentlessly.

But today, all that was gonna change. Owen had promised to bring a book that was sure to capture Jesse's imagination. It was about a time travelling super spy named Colton Tripp. Jesse couldn't wait to read it. He'd worry about how to get it home without Jacob seeing, later.

After breakfast, they met behind Jesse's house. As Jesse rounded the corner, he saw Owen but no book.

"Dude!" he said with disappointment, "Where's the book?"

Owen looked at him with an expression of guilt and something else. Fear?

"Um," Owen stammered, "I-I forgot it." Owen's shoulders sagged and he looked at the ground.

Seeing Owen's reaction made Jesse feel bad for bringing it up. Hoping to calm Owen down, he said, "Whoa, it's okay, dude. We can just run back to your house and grab it."

"NO!" Owen said quickly, with a scared, desperate look on his face. That's when Jesse noticed the collar on Owen's shirt seemed stretched, almost torn.

Startled by Owen's suddenly harsh tone, Jesse just stood and stared at him. Something just wasn't right. Owen lowered his gaze to the ground again and apologized, "Sorry, dude. It's just that my mom isn't home. Just...Tom."

Owen's stepdad. Not much was ever said about him, but Jesse got the impression that Owen didn't care for Tom and this pretty much solidified that feeling.

"Okay," Jesse said, eager to change the subject, "so whatcha wanna do then?"

Owen shrugged, but brightened slightly, probably equally glad to have the subject changed.

"I know!" Jesse exclaimed excitedly. ' "Let's go down to the creek," he said as he turned and ran across the field. Owen smiled and ran after him.

In the wooded area on the other side of the train tracks was a small creek that ran parallel to the tracks themselves.

Jesse led them to a spot where the creek widened. It had a rope swing hanging from a tree branch above the widest, and probably deepest, spot of the creek. The swing had a flat board attached to the end.

"Check it out," Jesse said proudly.

Owen got that sheepish look again. "It looks dangerous," he said quietly.

Now it was Jesse's turn to lower his head. Seriously, did this kid have NO sense of adventure?

Jesse sighed, as he found himself doing a lot lately, and looked up at Owen once more. He squinted his eyes as he stared intently at Owen.

"Don't...move," Jesse whispered as he crept closer to Owen, who immediately had a look of intense terror on his face.

"W-w-what is it?" Owen stammered. Jesse searched the ground for a stick as he quietly said, "There is a HUGE scorpion on your shoulder!"

With those words the small creek and wooded area started to change. The creek slowly morphed into a wide river, complete with a wild and dangerous-looking set of rapids. The small grouping of trees became a huge expanse of forest. Vines hung from the canopy of trees that blocked the sky.

Owen's look of terror got even more intense. He wanted to scream and run, smacking his shoulders all the way but he knew that if he even moved, the scorpion would sting him.

Jesse was in front of Owen now, holding a sharp stick. He brought it level with Owen's face. "Okay, on three, you're gonna drop to your knees," Jesse said slowly.

Owen began to shake. "It's okay, it's okay!" Jesse said, trying to calm his friend. "Just do what I say."

Jesse began counting, "One..." The scorpion, enormous and as black as a starless night, seemed to sense that something was about to happen. It raised its tail in an offensive posture. It was going to strike.

"...Two, three!" Jesse said quickly, swinging the stick. Owen dropped in an instant and the scorpion found itself in midair just as the stick whacked it into a nearby tree. It hit with a crunch, falling to the ground, dead.

That time Owen *did* scream. A loud high-pitched yell of terror blending into frustration. It echoed through the forest, scattering birds and other animals.

"Don't DO that!" Owen yelled at Jesse. Both boys were breathing heavily. Jesse, finally able to breathe, said, "I'm sorry but I had to. If I hadn't," he continued, "you'd be a dead man and we've come too far to let something like a scorpion sting stop us." Jesse pleaded.

"Yeah, but a little warning would be nice when you're gonna...you know," Owen said.

Confident that he'd made his point, Owen nodded his head, finally on board with the imaginary adventure. Jesse reached into a satchel hanging from his hip that Owen didn't remember seeing there a minute ago. Jesse pulled out a large blue crystal. "We finally have the Jewel of the Three Hearts," he said slowly, "and as you know, with this, we can save the world."

His expression changed from hopeful to intense, stern. "But we have to get out of this forest first," Jesse pointed to the river, "and THAT, is all that stands in our way."

Jesse put the jewel back in his satchel as he stood up and moved to the river's edge. He wiped his brow as he surveyed the area. "I think if we ran and jumped, we could reach that vine and swing across," he said, pointing to vine.

Owen, now standing beside Jesse, looked doubtful. Jesse noticed his expression. "Don't suppose you have any better ideas?"

Owen thought a minute, looking up and down the river. There were no downed trees that they could use to cross. He finally shook his head, indicating he could think of nothing better.

"Then let's do this," Jesse said as he started to back up, never taking his eyes off of the vine. "I'll go first." Owen moved out of the way, ready to see how it was done.

Jesse took a deep breath and ran toward the river. He reached the bank and, in one fluid motion, jumped. He reached the vine and grabbed it tightly as his momentum carried him forward.

He landed safely on the opposite side. He let go of the vine and bent at the waist with his hands on his knees, catching his breath. After a few seconds, he stood and turned around. He gave Owen a sly smile and a shrug and said, "See? Nothin' to it."

Owen gulped and looked one last time for another way across. Again, nothing.

He backed up, looked at the river, decided he might need even more room so he took a few more steps back.

After a few minutes psyching himself up, he started running toward the river. "This is crazy, this is crazy, this is crazy," Owen said as he ran the last few steps to the river bank.

He planted his right foot and pushed off, sending himself hurtling toward the vine.

His hands reached out and for a split second he thought he wasn't going to make it. Then he felt the vine in his hands, and he felt himself swinging toward the far bank, where Jesse stood waiting.

Owen's feet hit the edge just as Jesse grabbed the vine. Owen teetered for what seemed like minutes until Jesse reached for his hands.

Jesse had released the vine to reach for him and in that split second, Owen lost what little balance he'd managed to find. Their fingertips touched briefly as Owen started to wave his arms frantically, trying to regain his balance.

The water rushed up to consume him as he fell backward. Jesse was left reaching as he watched the rapids take his friend away

"Owen!" Jesse yelled as he ran in the direction that the rapids had taken Owen.

"Jesse!" Owen sputtered, fighting to keep his head above water.

Jesse ran along the bank of the river, struggling to keep Owen in his sights. He could see his friend trying to swim, but the rapids were just too strong.

Finally, Owen came to a bend in the river and was able to get to a low-hanging branch from a tree. He held tight as Jesse caught up to him.

Jesse stood on the bank smiling as Owen struggled to hold onto the branch. He was slipping as he said to Jesse, "Why are you smiling?"

Jesse started to laugh. "Um, dude...stand up."

As Owen was thinking just how impossible the notion of standing up was, the rapids began to slow. The banks of the river began to move inward. The immense vastness of the forest shrank until it was once again just a small wooded area.

Owen found himself sitting in no more than six inches of water, and standing up was no longer an impossible task.

Jesse was laughing now as Owen climbed out of the creek. He offered a hand but Owen refused. After all, it *was* only ankle deep.

Still, Owen was NOT amused. It wasn't like he could go home like this. He couldn't face Tom with his clothes soaked. Tom had gotten furious over far less, and Owen had no intention on finding out what Tom's next level of anger was.

Jesse and Owen made their way out of the woods. Once clear of the trees, they found themselves by the railroad tracks. They turned toward the direction of home and started walking.

"'Well, that was fun, huh?" Jesse said with a chuckle. Owen, not seeing the humor in his friend's statement, stopped walking and stared at hole through Jesse. "What?" Jesse asked, not knowing what the big deal was.

Owen's gaze shifted slightly. Jesse, realizing that his friend was no longer looking at him, followed Owen's line of sight and realized just what Owen was looking at.

A huge, rundown barn stood next to the tracks. Jesse had never been down this far so he'd never seen it before. "Whoa...!" both boys said in unison.

They walked to the barn and up to the front door. It was a big sliding door that looked like it hadn't been moved in years. The boys tried moving it, but it was extremely heavy.

"Okay, let's try again," Jesse told Owen, "but this time, put all your weight into it." They tried once again and this time, the door lurched forward with a horrible screech. It only moved a couple feet but it was enough for the boys to slip through...but they didn't move.

"Go ahead." Jesse said calmly, "I'll stand watch." Owen stared at Jesse for a beat and then shifted his gaze to the darkness beyond the door. He couldn't bring himself to speak so he just quickly shook his head.

Jesse's calm demeanor melted away as he realized that he'd have to go first if they were going to go on this adventure. "Fine," he sighed, "I'll go first...but you better stay close behind me."

The musty smell hit Jesse as he slowly stepped inside. He couldn't see much of anything at first. The light from the open door helped a bit as Jesse, with Owen close behind, crept further into the barn.

The floor was covered in dirt and hay so they didn't make much noise as they walked. Owen managed to resist the urge to reach out and grab hold of Jesse for comfort. But just barely.

Sunlight from a second-floor window was helping illuminate the contents of the barn and as their eyes slowly adjusted, they could make out some of the stuff. Old seats from cars, stacks of rotting wood, dresser drawers just laying in a heap, old shutters leaning against the wall. Dusty shelves held a multitude of items, equally covered in dust. There were cabinets mounted to the walls, some with doors and some without.

Being able to see, however slightly, helped them feel more comfortable so they broke up and started looking around separately.

Jesse went to the wall and started looking in the cabinets. They were filled with rusty old tools, ancient cans of oil, and other containers filled with nails and screws.

"Um, Jesse?" Owen said quietly. Jesse turned from the cabinets and at first couldn't see Owen. Then the sound of Owen's voice helped Jesse pinpoint his friend's location. From the back of the barn, he heard, "You might wanna come see this."

Jesse found Owen standing in the doorway to a separate room. He peered over Owen's shoulder into the room. There, bathed in a cascade of sunlight from another window, stood an ancient looking tractor. Dust particle twinkled in the sunlight.

The boys were in absolute awe. They felt as if they'd stumbled on a treasure. Jesse walked into the room and right up to the tractor. He ran a hand down the side and made a streak in the dust.

They each took turns sitting on the tractor for a bit until Jesse finally said, "You know what, Owen?"

Owen paused his investigation of the tractor and looked at Jesse. "This should be our HQ!" Jesse said excitedly.

"Yeah!" Owen concurred.

"Just think of all the adventures we can have here!" Jesse continued, "We should just clean it up a bit and then come back tomorrow with some supplies."

For the next hour or so, they worked hard at rearranging the old car seats into a living area, complete with a coffee table made out of an old wooden crate.

After they got the living area just the way they liked it, they both collapsed onto their "couch" and surveyed their handiwork. Both boys were out of breath.

As they made a list of things to bring back tomorrow to spruce up their new headquarters, they noticed the light was slowly diminishing. It was getting late.

On the way out, Jesse and Owen made sure to slide the door closed to make it look as though no one had been there.

They talked excitedly all the way home about how cool they were going to make their fort.

As they finally made it back to the field behind the trailer park, Jesse said to Owen, "Make sure you don't forget all the stuff tomorrow."

Owen smiled and said, "Don't worry, I won't."

Jesse rounded the corner of his trailer but a second later his head popped back. "Oh and bring that book tomorrow too," he said.

Chapter Six

The next morning, Owen finished his breakfast, grabbed the backpack that he had filled with supplies the night before, and made for the door. Just before he walked out, he remembered the book. He went to his room, shoved the book into the backpack and returned to the front door.

He closed his front door behind him, ran down the steps...and came to a screeching halt.

Standing less than three feet from him was Tom. Apparently, Tom was going to wash his car, again. This time by hand because he was carrying a bucket, filled with sudsy water, and a huge sponge.

Tom had stopped and was staring a hole through Owen. "Where you think you're going, boy?" he asked.

Owen, frozen in place at the foot of the steps, stammered, "Uhhhh...I-I was going to meet Jesse."

Tom snickered, "Oh, you don't have plans? Good," he said sarcastically. He held the bucket out to Owen.

Owen didn't move at first.

Tom glared at him and continued to hold the bucket out.

Owen, realizing that is was useless to resist, put his backpack down, and took the bucket and sponge. Tom turned around and said, "I'll get the hose." He walked toward the shed at the back of the trailer.

Owen sighed, looked over at Jesse's house, and then walked to Tom's car. He placed the bucket down and put the sponge in the water. Once it was soaked, he took the sponge and got started scrubbing the car.

Tom walked up a few minutes later, carrying the hose and a folding chair. He hooked the hose up to the water and then sat down on the chair. He sat there staring at Owen. He nodded once, as if to say "keep going," so Owen kept scrubbing.

For the next half hour, Owen scrubbed the car under the watchful eye of his stepfather. Owen had tried to hurry, but Tom would have none of it. Tom didn't speak, other than to indicate that Owen had missed a spot.

Owen was almost finished scrubbing the car when Jesse came walking up. "Hey dude, I thought we were meeting," Jesse said casually, not noticing Tom sitting there at first.

"He's busy," Tom grumbled. Jesse jumped, startled. He looked at over at the man sitting there, then back at Owen.

Owen, his back partially to his stepfather, silently mouthed one work to Jesse, *"Tom."* With that one word, Jesse understood the situation he'd wandered into.

"So, are you almost done?" Jesse asked.

"He's done when I say he's done," Tom said to Jesse.

Jesse's mind raced. "I'll help if you have another sponge," he offered to Owen, *not* Tom. Owen looked expectantly at Tom, hoping that the man hadn't noticed Jesse's intentional break in etiquette.

But Tom *had* noticed. He was glaring at Jesse, and Jesse was glaring right back at Tom. They stood like that for what seemed like hours.

Finally Jesse, perhaps realizing that he was no match for a grown man, looked away.

Tom stood up slowly and walked up to the Jesse but when he spoke, he was addressing Owen, "Boy, you better teach your friend some manners."

When Tom finally looked at him, a chill raced down Owen's spine. He knew he was in trouble, but surprisingly, Tom said, "Now git...and be back *before* dark for once."

Owen grabbed his backpack, and the boys ran to the field. Jesse retrieved his own backpack from where he'd stashed it.

Soon the boys were walking on the train tracks and halfway to the barn before they spoke. It was Jesse who broke the silence. "Did you remember the book?" he asked.

Owen nodded, but said nothing.

They walked in silence for a while until Jesse once again spoke, "Yeah so, your stepdad's kind of a jerk, huh?"

Owen glanced at his friend, who was now looking at him with a huge smile on his face.

Both boys started laughing. They laughed so hard and for so long that they were out of breath when they reached the barn. They were both glad to have the tension relieved though.

They walked up to the barn and slid the door open. They removed their backpacks and took out their flashlights. They clicked the flashlights on and walked inside. Everything was just the way they had left it.

In the living room, they began placing supplies on the coffee table. Crackers, cookies, powdered drink mix and water, etc. They also brought paper plates and plastic cups.

Owen retrieved the book from his backpack and sat down on the couch. To help them see, they'd brought candles and a book of matches. Jesse sat next to Owen, lit a candle and placed it on the coffee table.

They opened the book, placed it on the table in front of the candle, and Owen began to read aloud, "*Colton Tripp, Man of Time - Volume One.*"

> *Agent Colton Tripp stood very still in the middle of the lab. He held his breath, along with everyone else in the room, and waited. The seconds passed, slow as molasses through a pinhole.*
>
> *Everyone in the room, scientists, assistants, other agents, were all staring at the same empty spot at the back of the lab. From behind the relative safety of the bulletproof glass, of course.*
>
> *Though they'd all been waiting, the sudden flash of light made them jump.*
>
> *The flash was followed a split second later by a loud boom, and then the time machine was there, in the same spot it had been a few minutes before.*

Owen continued reading as Jesse stood and looked around. He shined his flashlight toward the tractor and it began to change. The rust and old brown paint fell to the ground and was replaced with the glow of shining steel. The tractor itself seemed to smooth itself into the shape of the time machine.

It was longer than the tractor had been, a little taller, and round. The spot where the seat of the tractor had been was now a control panel with a seat of its own right in front of it. The whole machine was enclosed in a glass bubble and had two "engines" on the sides. They were the capsules that contained the glowing pink gel that was used to propel the machine, and its pilot, through time.

Jesse smiled as he slowly turned and took in the intricate detail of the lab, in which he and Owen now stood.

"Wow!" Owen exclaimed as he walked forward to stand next to his friend. "This is amazing." All around the lab were computer stations within the walls with people sitting in front of them hurriedly tapping keyboards.

The friends stood and stared as scientists and lab assistants rushed around the room, yelling orders and instructions. In the midst of all of the chaos, Owen noticed that they were both now wearing futurific silver suits.

A man in a lab coat ran up to Jesse and adjusted something on the front of Jesse's suit. "Two minutes, Sir," he said as he inserted a small chip into the contraption strapped to Jesse's chest. With that, the man in the lab coat scurried off.

Jesse looked at Owen. "Sir?"

Owen smirked at his friend, "Colton Tripp. remember?" Jesse nodded understanding. "You're kind of a big deal around here," Owen said with a smile.

"And I am your faithful friend Steve Jordan," Owen said proudly. He leaned a little closer to Jesse, "I kinda go wherever you go but..."

Jesse, *Colton*, looked skeptical, "But what?'

"Well," Owen, *Steve*, continued, "Steve isn't the brightest guy...but he's *loyal*." With that, Colton seemed to understand where this was going. He was the "big deal" time traveling spy with a "not so bright sidekick."   "Well, this should be fun." he said.

Another scientist came rushing forward and ushered the two men toward the time machine. "It's time, gentleman." The scientist opened the door to the machine and stood aside to allow the time travelers access.

Colton and his *loyal* friend, Steve, boarded the time machine. Before closing the door to the machine, the scientist motioned to a computer in front of them, "Your briefing."

Steve reached for the computer as the door closed. His fingers danced across the keyboard as he called up the mission briefing.

Colton waited in the pilot's seat as Steve read over the details of the mission. He started to get impatient and asked, "So how far into the future are we going?"

Steve, still reading, held up his hand, palm toward Colton.

After another minute of silence, Steve finished reading and said aloud, "It looks like we're going into the PAST actually."

"The Past?" Colton was as surprised as Steve sounded.

"Well, kind of." Steve continued. Colton gave his friend a quizzical look.

"It's the past from where we are *now*," Steve said. "You see, we're *in* the year 3245. We're *going* to the year 2366 to stop a catastrophic event from happening."

Colton considered it all for a moment, while Steve read the briefing again. Finally Colton asked, "So let me make sure I have this right. I'm *from* the year *2016* but I'm *in* the year 3245 and I'm *going* to the year 2366?"

Steve nodded but didn't look at him.

"Okay...so what's this Event?" Colton asked.

As Steve finished reading the file for the second time, he swallowed hard and closed his eyes. "The event we have to stop is being perpetrated by someone that you've faced before," Steve began as he opened his eyes and looked at Colton. Something in the mission briefing had obviously upset him.

"His name is Dr. Tyler Young. Just over five years ago, you stopped him from releasing a gas over Old New York City." Steve continued. "The gas would have turned everyone into mindless zombies that would have done anything that Dr. Young told them to," Steve explained.

Colton said, "Okay, so we stop him again. What's the big deal?'

Steve, still looking at Colton, said, "There's more..." He looked back to the computer screen, "Apparently he's held such a grudge against you that this time he took his own time machine and went back to the year 2366 to cause the catastrophic event."

Confused, Colton asked, "Yeah but what does that have to do with *me?*"

"Well, you see," Steve said, "he's perfected a sort of makeshift bomb using nothing but items commonly found around the house...and vinegar."

Colton stared at Steve, "Vinegar?"

Steve looked up from the computer into Colton's eyes, then back at the screen, then shrugged, "Um, that's what it says..."

"But...what...does...it...have to do with *ME?*" Colton said slowly, starting to get frustrated.

Steve said, "Colton, he's going to use the bomb to blow up your family. Like, your *whole* family." Steve let that sink in and then continued, "In 2366, your family had a reunion and every known living member attended. Dr. Young is going to wipe your whole family out of existence."

Colton sat staring at Steve for a few seconds, his mind racing. Then he turned back toward the front and said, "Then let's go stop him...but this time," he turned back to Steve, an intense look on his face, "we stop him for good."

A few minutes later, after a countdown and another flash, they were heading back to the year 2366. Outside the ship, the time streams flew by in waves of color. It was beautiful, but they hardly noticed. They travelled in silence for what seemed like hours but in truth had only been a few minutes. With Colton's newly found intensity, brought on by the very idea of his whole family being killed, their trip now had an ominous tone that made everything else besides getting there, seem secondary.

The time streams had begun to slow as they neared their destination and then the color faded leaving nothing but white light.

With a faint popping sound, they had arrived in a blinding white flash.

The white light dimmed and was suddenly replaced by green. Steve found himself looking at the green substance intently until he realized just *what* he was looking at. Leaves. He was looking at leaves pressed up against the glass. The ship was in a bush or bushes.

Steve engaged the cloaking device so no unsuspecting person happened by and saw it in the bushes and they exited the ship.

Colton surveyed his surroundings. Everything looked normal enough. They were in what seemed to be a park of some kind. A grouping of tables was set up in the middle of it, and everything looked nicely decorated.

A few women were setting up chairs while a man carried a box about the size of a loaf of bread to the center of the tables. He set it on the ground and took a few steps back. He aimed a controller of some kind at the box and suddenly, a light shot out of it. The light spread up and out until it formed a canopy covering all of the tables. The light "tent" came complete with tied up sides that could be put in place in case the weather turned bad.

Steve chuckled, elbowed Colton in the side gently, and said, "That's the future, buddy."

They continued to watch as more people began to show up. The people carried various boxes and plates of food, but Colton ignored all of that. Instead, he studied their faces. He was amazed to see the resemblance he shared with them all. Sure, in some it was slight. The setting of the eyes, their hair color, the placement of the nose. There was no denying it. These people were his descendants. His *family*. And they were all going to die unless he helped them.

Colton and Steve retreated back to their ship, still nestled in the bush, cloaked.

They left the cloaking device engaged while they sat in the ship and devised a plan. The bomb would explode in just under three hours but the biggest problem they faced was they had no idea where Dr. Young was hiding out. That left them with no other option than to search the park.

They split up and spent the next few hours circling the park, staying in contact with each other via a small microphone in the collar of their shirt and an even smaller ear piece implanted deep inside their ear.

On each pass around the park, Colton veered a little closer to the party. Though most of the people shared some similar features, Colton was drawn to one woman in particular. She was very old and remained seated pretty much the whole time. She had a seemingly endless line of people from the party coming up and greeting her.

Colton realized that she must be the eldest member of the family which made her the closest to him. He studied her face as closely as he could while trying to look inconspicuous. It was so obvious that the old woman was his descendant that it made it extremely difficult to look away.

This mission was unlike any other. He'd never had a mission this personal. Feelings were coursing through Colton that threatened to rip him apart. He'd never felt anything like it. This was his family and if he failed this mission, they were all dead.

Just then, Steve spoke to him through the earpiece, "I think I got something. Southeast corner of the park."

Colton quickened his pace until he was moving at a fast walk. Running would seem out of place and might alert the partygoers which, in turn, would prevent him from stopping Dr. Young for good.

Colton spotted Steve, who was looking up at something that Colton couldn't see at first. He followed Steve's line of sight and saw a man in coveralls hovering in the air, riding a column of air. The man held a small hose that was attached to his backpack. He seemed to be watering all of the vegetation from above.

Colton walked up to Steve, "A gardener. Very suspicious!"

Steve didn't look away, "Just watch."

The two men stood perfectly still, watching the gardener. For a while, nothing happened. The gardener just floated along on his jetstream, watering flowers and such. Then he casually looked over his shoulder at the party. When he turned back, he spoke into some sort of communicator he had in his sleeve.

Colton started to get a sinking feeling. "So now we know Young has at least one person helping him pull this off," he said, but Steve wasn't paying attention anymore. At first, Colton didn't understand just what had taken Steve's attention away but then he saw it too.

All around the park were more gardeners, all floating on streams of air, pretending to work while secretly watching the party. Colton counted seven others and all of them were spraying the bushes and trees just like the first. "We're in trouble," Steve said quietly.

As the gardeners finished, they moved along the row of trees. Colton looked at his watch. He was opening his mouth to tell Steve that they still had almost an hour before the blast was supposed to happen, when he heard a loud explosion from the opposite end of the park.

The explosion had come from a trash bin nowhere near Colton's family so it was pretty easy to deduce that this bomb wasn't the main threat. But if that bomb had just been the opening act, they still didn't know when the main attraction was going to happen...or just what the main attraction even was.

What the trash bomb was successful in doing was causing fear and chaos. A large group of panicked people, including Colton's family members, were sent running deeper into the park. They were running straight toward the areas that had just been sprayed by the gardeners, who were now nowhere to be seen.

As the scared mob of people flooded the central area of the park, two more small explosions erupted at either edge and trees began bursting into flame. The people were forced to run down a path with burning trees on either side of them.

Colton suddenly realized what was happening. The crowd was being herded. The explosions were timed to go off in sequence to steer them all to the same spot and the trees were to keep people from straying away from the path that lead them to...Colton ran ahead to see where they were going. The Lake.

The lake area was the biggest wide open area. It made sense. This was the best way to cause the most amount of damage when the main attraction happened.

Colton's mind raced. He had minutes, *maybe*, to save these people, most of which were his family. No ideas were coming to mind as of yet. The herd of terrified people was headed right toward him so he did the only thing he could think of: he stretched his arms out wide and stood his ground. He waved his hands vigorously and yelling at the top of his lungs, "Not this way! The other way!"

It was no use. No one could hear him over the sounds of their own screams. The crowd just parted and ran around him.

As they passed, Colton called Steve. They'd gotten separated in all the commotion. "Steve! They're being lead down to the lake."

After only a fraction of a second, Steve replied, "That can't be good. Let's get down there."

Colton took off at top speed toward the lake. He managed to pass most of the scared people, who started to slow down as they realized that they didn't know where to go next.

As Colton reached the lakefront, everything seemed calm. Some birds took flight in the distance, having been startled by all the commotion. He, just like the rest of the people filling in around him on the sand, had no idea what to do next.

Then a thought came to him. If Dr. Young wanted the mass of people to come this way, then the way out of this was to go back the way they'd come. Colton turned around and yelled at the top of his lungs, "Everyone, listen to me. You have to go back!"

By this time, Steve had come running up to him and seemed to understand. He attempted to help get the people to turn around and head back the way they had come, but seeing as it was still engulfed in flame, they had no intention of going along with that plan.

Colton and Steve kept pleading with the people to turn around but by this time, it was almost impossible. The people felt safer just standing at the edge of the lake. Most had already turned to watch the trees burn, sure that the worst had already happened.

Winded from all of the yelling, Colton stopped to take a breath and found himself face to face with the old woman from the family reunion. She was terrified but seemed calmer than most of the others.

They stared at each other in a moment that seemed to last forever until her eyes shifted to something behind Colton, and widened in fear.

Colton turned quickly and immediately saw what had scared her. A large fin had started to rise out of the water. It was dark green in color and was attached to the top of a huge fish, or more accurately, a huge submarine in the *shape* of a fish.

As he looked closer, Colton could see someone at the controls inside the eye of the *fish*. It was Dr. Young, Colton was sure.

As the huge machine rose to the surface, the hundreds of bystanders stood and stared. Then it began to turn silently towards the crowd, and that's when the fact that they were in danger began to set in.

As if a silent alarm had gone off, the crowd turned and began running the opposite way, the way they'd originally come. Colton was knocked off his feet by the sudden exodus as the people pushed and shoved to escape whatever the giant mechanical fish was going to do.

From the ground, Colton looked up, dazed. The air was filled with smoke from the previous explosions and the trees that continued to burn. He tried to yell out, to tell the people to hurry, but he choked on the words.

Suddenly, Steve was there, kneeling in front of him. Steve leaned down and shook Colton by the shoulders, "Dude, I have to go home."

Colton didn't understand just what Steve was saying. Was it a code of some sort?

"Jesse! I have to get going, dude."

The story gradually disappeared. The lake. The people. The park. All gone. They were back in the barn. Jesse was lying on the floor, covered in dust and hay and Owen was kneeling in front of him.

"Oh. Well, to be continued, I guess." he said as he stood up and brushed himself off, feeling a bit foolish. It was kind of an anti-climatic end to their day, and the first time they had ever *not* finished a story.

"Sorry, dude. Tom told me to be back before dark," Owen said.

Jesse finished brushing off and grabbed his backpack. He put the Colton Tripp book in it and said, "Okay, let's go then."

Together, they walked home. In no hurry since it wasn't dark yet. They talked casually about the story and how they'd finish it tomorrow, but overall, the thought of Tom weighed heavily on them both.

Chapter Seven

The next morning, Jesse shot out of bed, excited to meet Owen and head back to the barn.

He'd stayed up late last night reading more about Colton Tripp's adventures, and now he couldn't wait to get there.

He quickly got dressed and retrieved the book. He grabbed a Pop-Tart from a kitchen cupboard and was almost to the front door when he noticed Jacob sitting in the living room.

Jesse stopped cold. As far as he could tell, Jacob was ignoring him, as usual.

He slowly began walking toward the door, trying to look inconspicuous. He risked one last look over his shoulder as he reached for the door handle and saw Jacob looking right at him.

Jacob's eyes flicked down to the book that Jesse held and then back up to Jesse's face. A slow smile began to form on Jacob's face. Jesse knew he was busted so he casually opened the door and walked out.

As he descended the stairs from his porch he thought to himself about all of the teasing that was sure to come when he got home.

Jesse ran to the usual meeting place, behind the trailer park, only to find that Owen wasn't there...again. He stood waiting for a few minutes but then the urge to get going made him run to Owen's house.

This time, no one was outside.

He mounted the porch steps in a flash and knocked on the door. No answer. He knocked again and waited. Everything seemed eerily quiet both outside and from inside the home.

Finally, the door opened, but only a few inches. Owen's mom peeked around the door, "Oh, hello, Jesse."

Jesse felt that something was wrong. "I-is Owen home?" he asked.

Owen's mom, her face only slightly visible from behind the barely opened door, said, "Yes, I'll go get him."

With that, she closed the door, but Jesse had finally realized what was wrong. It wasn't easy to see, but Owen's mother had a bruise on her cheek. Perhaps a black eye as well. She'd tried to keep that side of her face behind the door but had turned slightly to look towards Owen's room, and that's when Jesse had seen the bruise.

The door opened again, but this time it was Owen. He stepped outside onto the porch and made for the stairs without saying a word. Jesse said, "Wait, dude, is everything okay?'

Owen stopped as he reached the steps of the porch. He didn't turn around but said, "Yeah."

"It's just…," Jesse started but trailed off as Owen turned around.

"Everything is fine." Owen said, suddenly sounding a little *too* happy, "Let's go, dude." With that, Owen pushed his glasses up with his index finger, turned quickly and bounded down the stairs.

Jesse followed his friend, deciding to let it go. As he descended the stairs, he caught movement from the window where Owen's living room would be. A man's face looked out; it was Tom.

As Tom met his Gaze, another piece of the puzzle seemed to fall into place. Jesse didn't know what the puzzle *was* exactly, but he knew one thing for sure: Tom was *not* a nice man.

Jesse followed his friend to the field and to the tracks where they turned and began walking to the barn. Once again, they were silent. This time, Jesse didn't know what to say.

They walked all the way to the barn in silence.

Once there, they opened the door, lit their flashlights, and went inside, closing the door behind them.

They went to their couch and sat down, opening the book and lighting candles. Once their eyes were adjusted enough, Owen began reading, picking up where they left off the day before

Jesse lay down on the floor and was once again amazed as the wood planks covered in dust began to wither away as Owen read, replaced by soft green grass.

They were once again Colton and Steve, and they knew that this mission was going bad...quickly.

The air was filled with smoke and the sounds of people screaming. Colton yelled for the people to hurry as he turned himself over onto his backside. He started to get up but then he glanced to the lake.

The fish submarine had made its way to the shore and a man was walking down a ramp that had come out of the mouth of the fish. Dr. Young.

Dr. Young had long hair and wore glasses. He wore a long black trench coat and a cold evil smile. Colton locked eyes with him for a split second, then a loud screech took his attention away.

Having found no reason for the noise, Colton looked back to see Dr. Young on shore but something had changed. He was no longer wearing the trench coat.

The evil doctor continued walking up the shore, through the billowing smoke, toward Colton, but now he wore a familiar-looking jacket. Colton had seen it before but he couldn't place just where.

He looked back up at Dr. Young but now the face was different. Where the older face of the evil scientist had been was now replaced with the face of a teenager.

Suddenly, the world began to lose all color and texture. The greens of the park were gradually replaced with browns and greys. The adventure was gone, and they were once again in the old barn.

Still lying on the floor, Jesse had to blink a few times for his eyes to read-just to this new reality. He could hardly believe it, but he was staring at his brother, Jacob, standing where Dr. Young had been seconds before.

Jacob was standing just inside the barn, his friends Curtis and Tommy just behind him, peering inside. The three older boys surveyed the scene before them as they entered the barn.

Jesse stood and brushed himself off as Jacob walked up to him, smiling. "So, what's going on here, little brother?" Jacob asked.

Jesse stood silent, not knowing what to say. He turned to look behind him to see Owen slowly putting the book down on the table in front of the couch.

"Looks like we got a couple of little kids playing nerd games, to me," Curtis said. "Right, Tommy?"

Tommy, walking around the opposite side by the table, nodded in agreement as he reached for the Colton Tripp book. He picked it up quickly as Owen reached for it. Tommy slapped Owen's hands away as he tossed the book to Jacob.

Jacob caught the book and began to flip through it. A look of disgust slowly crept onto his face as he skimmed the pages. Finally, he slammed it shut and looked at Jesse.

He held the book out to Jesse and asked, "You into this stuff now?" Jesse, still not knowing what to say, shook his head. Jacob continued, "Nerd books? Nerd games? Really?'

Jacob shook his head, "We may not always get along, but I never thought of you as a nerd," Jacob explained. "You may be a bratty little brother, but I always thought you were at least a *little* cool," he said.

Jacob noticed Owen standing there and motioned to him. "And now you're even hanging out with losers like this."

He started flipping through the book again, looking disgusted as he did so. Then he stopped at a random page, glared up at Jesse, and tore the page from the book.

Owen rushed forward to protest his book being destroyed. The word "Stop" was beginning to form on his lips when Tommy stepped in front of him and rammed a fist into his stomach.

Time seemed to stand still for everyone. In that fraction of a second, Owen had time to think that getting punched in the stomach didn't hurt nearly as much as he'd imagined. Then the pain hit him. He doubled over, making a horrible gagging noise that continued as he dropped to his knees, then onto his side where he curled himself into a fetal position.

Jesse had turned and watched his friend get punched in the stomach. What seemed like a million emotions welled up inside him. All he could manage to say was "Hey!" as he saw Owen fall to the floor, but he stood frozen to the same spot in front of Jacob.

Jacob had stopped ripping the pages out of the book. He watched the scene unfold, and smiled. He walked around Jesse to where Owen lay, writhing in pain.

Jacob knelt down and held the book in front of Owen's face, "So this is yours, huh?" Owen just groaned lightly. Jacob slowly ripped another page out of the book, right in front of Owen. He looked up at Jesse and smiled. Jesse glared back at his brother "Leave him alone." Jesse intended it to sound firm but it came out as more of a plea.

Jacob stood and gave Jesse a hurt look. "Leave who alone? Oh, him?" he said, motioning toward Owen. With that, he kicked Owen, still doubled over from the previous blow, right in the stomach.

Jesse rushed forward and knelt at Owen's side. Owen's eyes were closed tight as he lay on his side clutching his stomach. He was making a hacking sound as his body rocked with dry heaves.

Jesse looked up from his friend to see Jacob toss the book over to Curtis, who in turn opened it and put one half under his left arm for leverage and began trying to tear it in half with his other hand. After a few tries, he gave up and started ripping pages out instead.

All three older boys were laughing as Curtis continued tearing pages out of the book and throwing them in the air. The floor of the barn was littered with torn pages.

Jacob moved to the makeshift furniture. He kicked the couch over and smashed the table.

He and Tommy then went to the counter where the younger boys had set up a kitchen area and began grabbing containers of water and food. They dumped some of the containers and tossed some into the air, spilling their contents. Various snacks and powdered drink mix littered the already filthy floor.

Jesse could think of nothing to say, nothing to do. Never in his wildest dreams did he think that this could happen. He had finally found a friend that he actually liked being around and now this. Jacob was ruining it, and worst of all, Jesse was at a loss on just how to stop it.

The commotion finally began to die down. The barn was an absolute wreck.

Jacob and his friends began to walk toward the door, satisfied with the chaos they'd created.

As he walked out the door, Jacob looked over his shoulder and smiled at Jesse and then shook his head one last time. Then they were gone.

Owen hacked again and then rolled away from Jesse. He slowly hefted himself to his knees and breathed heavily while trying to regain his composure.

"Are you okay?" Jesse asked. Owen didn't answer. He turned his head and stared at Jesse for a few seconds and then rose to his feet. He looked around at the mess and began to cry.

Jesse rose and walked toward him, but Owen quickly turned away while trying to brush away the tears.

"We can fix this," Jesse said quietly, trying to sound as upbeat as possible. Owen once again turned to him and stared without saying a word. Tears were still running down his face, but he made no attempt to wipe them away now.

Owen, still silent, looked away and began walking to the door. He reached it and stopped for a beat, without looking back. He stood there, silent, his back to Jesse. Then he walked out, making his way to the railroad tracks.

Jesse walked to the door and watched his friend start walking home, without him.

Quickly, Jesse closed the door, leaving the mess to be sorted out at a later time, and ran after Owen. Jesse caught up to him, and followed a few steps behind. He once again didn't know what to say so he remained silent.

They walked all the way home in silence. At first, Jesse wasn't sure that Owen even knew that he was there. He actually made obvious attempts to kick rocks loudly enough for Owen to hear but got no reaction from his friend.

They walked across the field to the trailers and up to Owen's.

Owen ascended the steps to his front door. Jesse followed but Owen walked into his house and slammed the door before Jesse was even at the top of the steps.

Jesse stood there, confused and hurt. He waited for awhile, but it soon became obvious that Owen wasn't going to come back out so he descended the stairs and walked home, thoroughly devastated by the events of the day.

Chapter Eight

Storm clouds had rolled in overnight. The morning had started out as a dreary, rainy day but was quickly escalating into a downright depressing, *stormy* day.

It was shortly before lunch time as Jesse's stomach was starting to rumble as loud as the thunder as he walked on the train tracks.

He had on a simple slicker with a hood, but he refused to put the hood up. The rain was coming down hard and he was soaked to the bone but still, the hood remained down.

A person like him *deserved* to get poured on. What kind of friend was he? He stood by and let his friend, his *only* friend, get beat up. A person like that probably deserved more than a little rain.

He walked along the tracks, barely even paying attention to just where he was going.

Despite not really knowing where he was going, he found himself in front of the barn. *Returning to the scene of the crime.*

He stood staring at the barn, afraid to go in. Perhaps he was afraid to come face to face with yesterday's carnage.

This morning, he'd tried calling Owen but was told by Owen's mom that he didn't want to talk. He'd then tried to eat some cereal, but his appetite just wasn't there so he ended up lying in bed for hours.

Now he found himself more than a mile from home, standing in front of the place he associated with one of the worst moments in his life.

He let out a huge sigh and made his way up to the door. He opened it and went inside.

Despite the low amount of light, everything seemed the same as they'd left it yesterday.

He walked around for a while, looking through the mess, until he found what he was looking for; his flashlight. He picked it up and turned it on. Now he could see enough to find what he'd *really* come here for.

He spent the next hour gathering up every page and remnant of the Colton Tripp book. Plenty of the pages were torn and tattered, but Jesse was confident that he'd found every scrap.

He carefully stuffed them in his backpack, which had been left behind yesterday as well.

After he packed the backpack, he debated on straightening up the barn but finally decided against it. It didn't seem right somehow. He and Owen had built this, their headquarters, and if it was even to be used again, only he and his friend should build it back up.

He picked up the backpack, slid it over his shoulders and made for the door of the barn. With one final look back, he began the walk home, with his hood up this time.

When he'd made it to the trailer park, he decided to stop by Owen's. It was still raining and he was soaked but he *had* to try again to apologize to his friend.

He mounted the steps and knocked on Owen's front door. After just a few seconds, Owen's mom answered.

She opened the door all the way and greeted him with a big smile. Jesse could see none of the bruise on her cheek that he was *sure* he'd seen the previous day. Maybe he'd imagined it.

"Hey, Jesse," she said.

"Hi, uh, Owen's mom. Is Owen here?" Jesse said, having to raise his voice slightly to be heard over the rain. He found himself hoping that she'd invite him in. After all, he *was* soaked.

"You know, Jesse," he smile fading slightly, "Owen... isn't feeling well. You shouldn't be out in this weather either. You'll catch a cold."

Jesse, not sure if he truly believed that Owen was really sick, could only manage, "Okay." He turned and walked down the steps.

As he got to the bottom, Owen's mom said, "Maybe he'll feel better tomorrow." Jesse didn't bother to respond. He just walked home and went in out of the rain.

As he was taking off his slicker and boots, he heard a voice say, "What's up, turd?" It was his brother, sitting on the couch, watching TV.

As if his day hadn't been bad enough, now he had to deal with Jacob. He decided to try to just get to his bedroom as quickly as he could.

"So, where have you been all day? Getting a library card? You know, cause you're a bookworm now and all."

Jesse stopped and stared at his brother. "You know, Jacob," he began, finally having enough, "when I was younger, I used to look up to you. I used to want to be like you."

Jacob had stopped watching TV and was glaring at Jesse. "But now," Jesse continued, "I just feel sorry for you. You seem like you pretty much have it all. You're popular and have lots of friends...but you're the most miserable person I know."

With that, Jesse walked to his bedroom, hearing his brother say, "Whatever, nerd," as he went.

Once in his room, he spent the rest of the day working on his new project. The Colton Tripp book was in rough shape, but he had to try.

Some of the pages were torn cleanly out of the book, but others were ripped into multiple pieces.

Jesse spent hours painstakingly taping each page together, making sure the lines lined up so the reader could actually read the story.

There were a few times that the tear made it impossible to read the word so once that section was taped, Jesse took a pen and carefully wrote the letters back in.

All in all it was an incredibly tedious process, but it gave Jesse a chance to think about just what was important in his life.

A rainy day had always meant that he'd be stuck inside by himself, but today, it was different. He was stuck inside once again, by himself, but knowing his friend Owen was just down the street and didn't want to talk to him made him feel something he'd not felt before. He felt lonely.

The loneliness, combined with the feelings of regret at his own actions yesterday, was too much to bear.

He'd always thought that having friends was pretty low on the ladder of importance but after meeting Owen, and being taught so much by him in their rather short friendship, he was starting to rethink his ideas.

He had to fix this. He had to get his friend back so he doubled his efforts with the book. He hoped that repairing the book would be the first step in repairing his friendship.

After a long time working on the book, he looked toward the window and was surprised to see what little of the sun that had decided to show itself today, had started to diminish.

He quickly finished the last page and jumped up. He was determined to get this resolved today. Tomorrow was July Fourth, and he really wanted to celebrate the holiday with Owen.

He made his way to the kitchen and was pleased to see that Jacob was no longer in the living room. Jesse retrieved a plastic grocery bag from the cabinet under the sink and wrapped it around the book.

He put his boots and slicker back on and went outside only to be surprised that the rain had stopped. Maybe that meant good news for the fireworks tomorrow.

Jesse walked down to Owen's house but avoided the front door. Instead, he crept quietly to Owen's bedroom window, which was dark but for a small light, probably from lamp.

He stood on his toes and tapped on the window. No response so he tapped again, louder this time. This time, the curtain slowly moved aside and Owen's face appeared.

Jesse, pleased to see his friend, smiled and waved enthusiastically. Owen stared a moment and then lowered the curtain back into place. Jesse's smile faded. This wasn't going to be easy.

Jesse tapped again, louder still. The curtain moved aside again, quickly this time. Owen's face was there once again, but now it looked angry.

Jesse quickly held up the book before Owen could close the curtain again. As Owen noticed the book, Jesse smiled again and motioned for him to open the window.

Owen unlatched the window and pushed it open a little.

Jesse quickly took advantage of the moment, "Before you say anything, dude...I am *SO* sorry." He stopped a moment to gather his thoughts. "I want you to know that you are the best friend I've ever had, and I'm sorry I didn't act like it yesterday," he began, "I don't know what happened to me, but I made the wrong choice by not doing anything."

Jesse held the book out to Owen, who took it. "I fixed it the best I could. If you still want to be friends, I promise...that I'll...well, I'll be a better friend this time."

Owen looked at the pages, heavily taped, and smiled. He looked down at Jesse, pushed his glasses up with a finger, and nodded, "I guess that sounds okay."

Owen started to get tears in his eyes, "Jesse, I'm not so good at this stuff either. I've never had a friend even half as good as you. I don't know what a true friend should *be* so when that happened yesterday, all I could think was that it was somehow *MY* fault and if I'd have been a better friend, you'd have stuck up for me."

Jesse began to get tears in his own eyes. He couldn't stand seeing his friend cry and knowing that Owen blamed himself for his action, or lack of action, made it even worse.

"Owen, it wasn't your fault. I used to look up to Jacob and would have done anything to be accepted by him.," Jesse explained, trying to blink away the tears. "All of that came flooding back when he came to the barn. I don't know why but I just couldn't move."

Suddenly, Owen said, "Shhhhh..." and quickly closed the curtain.

Jesse ducked down, though in all actuality he didn't need to. He was low enough below the window that he couldn't be seen by anyone unless they opened the curtain and deliberately looked for him.

There was a new voice from inside the room. "Who you talkin to, boy?" Jesse knew the voice. It was Tom.

"I told you I wanted quiet while your momma ain't home."

Owen was silent. He knew by now not to disagree with his stepfather.

Tom looked around the room. He casually moved the curtain aside but didn't bother to look down so he never saw Jesse.

"Well," Tom said, letting the curtain fall back into place, "you might as well start getting ready for bed. You're gonna wash my car tomorrow morning. Early. And this time, that bratty friend of yours better not come around."

He left the room, closing the door behind him. Owen rushed back to the window and looked down. "Jesse." he whispered.

Jesse popped up suddenly, scaring Owen. Jesse chuckled a little but then his mood changed. "I hate that guy," he said.

"You and me both," Owen agreed.

Jesse shook his head at the thought of Owen having to deal with Tom on a daily basis. Having to wash that car. And with that thought came another. No. *More* than just a thought. *A plan.*

Owen noticed the blank look on his friends face. Then he saw the familiar smile creep onto his face. The smile that meant trouble. "Uh-oh," Owen said.

"No. Wait," Jesse said, finally returning Owen's stare, "I've got a plan. Let's meet tomorrow. Around noon. Do you have any money?" Jesse was practically out of breath with excitement.

"Just some in my piggy bank," Owen replied.

Jesse stood up and looked at Owen. "Bring whatever you can spare. Meet me in the field tomorrow at noon and I'll explain," Jesse said quickly yet quietly. "This is a big one, dude."

Jesse backed away, but as he did, he kept eye contact with Owen. He pointed at his friend, "Tomorrow. Noon."

Owen closed the window and got ready for bed. As he climbed into bed, he couldn't help but be anxious. From the sound of it, Jesse had a big plan. Perhaps it was fitting that tomorrow was July Fourth.

Chapter Nine

July Fourth

Owen met Jesse in the field at 12:05 the next afternoon. Jesse had arrived long before Owen, and now he waited next to three cans of white paint. The same cans that they'd found almost three weeks prior.

Once Owen had settled down in the grass next to him, Jesse excitedly began laying out his plan.

It was an elaborate plan for revenge. Revenge on pretty much everyone that had made their lives hell over the past month or more.

Jesse laid it out for Owen, gave Owen a chance to ask questions, and then laid it out again, making the necessary changes as he went.

It began with using the money that they'd each brought to get their hands on the supplies they'd need to pull this thing off. That would require a trip to the Dub.

As they rose from the grass, Jesse grabbed two of the paint cans and Owen grabbed the other. They walked to Jesse's house and deposited the cans under his porch steps where no one would see them.

Then Jesse had Owen stay outside while he went inside for a sec. This part was critical for their alibi.

Not long after he'd gone inside, Jesse came running out with a huge smile on his face. "We're all set, dude. She was asleep, but I woke her up to ask her. She said it was cool if you stayed the night."

Next they decided to go to Owen's house. Owen knew he had a much better chance of getting approval if Tom wasn't there. Luckily, after having Owen wash his car, he'd decided to go somewhere.

Owen's mom said he could stay the night at Jesse's. Everything was falling into place.

"So who is this 'Dub' guy?" Owen asked.

"His name is Trevor Thompson actually but over time, people started calling him T-double." Jesse began, "Then just 'double' and then that was shortened to 'Dub' as he started getting his business going.

"Like I told you before, he's the guy you go see when you want something. He runs his business out of his shed."

Owen started to get nervous. This whole thing sounded...shady. Dangerous even. He still had time to back out but he kept walking.

He knew he had to start taking more chances in life. He'd been playing it safe for this long and he was tired of it. Tired of bullies like Jacob and his friends walking all over him.

They were a few streets from theirs when Jesse walked up to a trailer and around to the back. He stepped up to the shed and knocked.

"Yo!" was the reply.

Jesse opened the door and motioned Owen to walk in. Owen hesitated. Jesse rolled his eyes and stepped through the door himself. Owen followed... after a deep breath.

The inside had a light, and the walls were lined with shelves. The shelves were heavily stocked with items. Candy, energy drinks, dirty magazines, lighters, cigarettes, boxes of fireworks, etc...

"Sup, Dub?" Jesse said casually. The Dub looked up from his magazine and gave a slight nod. "Um, lemme get a couple packs of jumping jacks, two packs of bottle rockets, a roman candle and a lighter...oh and a pack of Bubble Lubble," Jesse said.

Dub retrieved the items and put them in a recycled plastic grocery bag.

"Ten bucks." Dub said.

Jesse slowly stepped aside and motioned for Owen to step up, "Ten bucks."

Owen, trying to look casual, fumbled in his pocket and took out a hand full of crumpled dollar bills and change and held it out to Jesse.

Jesse gave Dub an embarrassed smile, helped Owen count it out, and handed the money over.

Once they'd received their items, they ran back to Jesse's house. They spent the whole afternoon planning.

Jesse's mom poked her head in at around 5:30 and asked them if they wanted dinner. Owen politely declined. He said he had to run home and get his stuff for the sleep over.

While Owen was gone, Jesse ate dinner with his mom. Jacob was staying the night with Curtis so it was just the two of them.

They didn't talk much, and when they did, it was mostly just small talk. Jesse's mom didn't have to work that night, and she asked him what he and Owen had planned. Jesse nearly choked on his bite of chicken until he remembered that she had no idea about the real plan so he just told her that they were gonna hang out and play *Bug Annihilator*.

As Jesse was finishing his dinner, he realized that he'd forgotten something so he casually got up, walked over to the pantry, and retrieved a set of keys.

"What are you doing?" his mother asked.

"Um, I need to get something from the shed." he answered.

"All right," she said, shrugging, "I don't know what you could possibly need from the shed, but okay."

The shed had been locked for a long time and held mostly stuff that had belonged to his dad. He knew that his mother couldn't bear to throw it out so when they'd moved here, she locked it up in the shed.

Curious, Jesse had gone in there a while back to check it out. He hadn't stayed long but he remembered seeing something he needed for tonight.

He unlocked the shed and went in. As he was rummaging through the boxes, he began to remember why he hadn't stayed too long the last time he'd come in here. Seeing his father's stuff kinda brought up a lot of feelings. Feelings that he had neither the time nor the urge to deal with right now.

He found the fishing line he'd come looking for, shut the light off, and padlocked the door back up.

As he was walking up the steps to his house, Owen came around the corner carrying his backpack.

The sun was going down, and they began to hear the first of what was sure to be a million fireworks going off that night.

"You ready, dude?" Jesse asked with a sly smile.

Owen let out a breath. "Yep, let's do this."

They went inside and ran to Jesse's bedroom to get ready. They also used this time to go over the plan again. Once they saw that the sun was completely down, they knew that Jacob and his friends would be getting started, and that meant it was time.

First, they changed clothes. Jesse wore black sweatpants and a long-sleeve black shirt. He took a T-shirt and stuck his face through the hole where his head was supposed to go. Then he wrapped the sleeves around his head and tied them. Once that part was done, he pulled the bottom portion of the head hole up over his mouth and nose.

The whole idea was to look like a ninja, and Owen had to admit, it wasn't bad.

Owen took out his outfit and began to change. He had a long-sleeve dark blue turtle neck shirt and a pair of black dress slacks.

Jesse stared at Owen in disbelief.

"What?" Owen said in a defensive tone.

"That's the best you could do?" Jesse asked.

"Yes!" Owen said, even more defensive now.

Jesse sighed. It would have to do so he helped Owen put his mask on.

They double checked the backpack they were taking with them and then climbed out the window. As Jesse helped him down, he said, "Still time to turn back. Are you sure you're ready?" Owen nodded. "Then it's go time," Jesse said.

They retrieved the paint cans and made their way to Owen's house. They set the cans up just like the plan dictated and then took another minute to compose themselves.

Jesse reached inside the backpack, pulled out a pack of jumping jacks and a lighter. He looked at his official digital *Bug Annihilator* wristwatch and saw that it was 9:45.

"Okay, I'm up," Jesse said. "Start getting the rest ready while I'm gone, but remember, this is the tricky part. I'm not sure where they're at exactly so I'm not sure how long it'll take. Just be ready."

"I'll be ready, dude." Owen said confidently. Jesse smiled. He liked this new out-for-revenge Owen.

They fist bumped, and then Jesse ran away.

He made his way toward Curtis' house, which was three streets over. He stayed in the shadows, mainly behind the trailers, and actually had fun being a "ninja."

As he was ready to cross over to Curtis' street, he heard a bottle rocket go off extremely close to him. He stopped and waited. Finally, another one went off from the direction of the clubhouse.

He ventured out onto the street so he could cross over to the parking lot of the clubhouse. He ran to the base of a small brick wall. It was only about three feet high and was there to separate the parking lot from the grass field next to the clubhouse.

He stayed crouched next to the wall and listened. He heard laughter and talking. He could tell that it was more than one person, but he couldn't tell who it was so he risked a quick peek over the wall.

It was Jacob with both Curtis and Tommy. Jesse silently gave a little "Yes!" Finding the older boys had been easier than he'd hoped.

He took out and unwrapped the pack of jumping jacks. He arranged them so he could have access to the wick but didn't separate them. He took out the lighter and prepared to light the wick.

He stopped to listen to the older boys. They were arguing now about who was going to light the next bottle rocket but they actually sounded like they'd gotten closer to him. Perfect.

Jesse made sure his mask was firmly in place, then slowly let out a breath, lit the fuse and counted to three. On three, he stood up and threw the whole pack of jumping jacks at his brothers feet.

The explosives went off practically all at once as all three of the boys danced around, trying to avoid the jumping sparks.

Jesse stood there for a few seconds, admiring his handy work. He wanted to remember the scared look on his brother's face.

As the last few jumping jacks were burning out, Jesse quickly turned and began running toward home. Not as fast as he could at first, though. He listened to make sure that the older boys were chasing him before he really turned on the speed.

He instantly regretted holding back because they were catching up to him...quickly. They were football players after all.

He was out of breath by the time he ran up to his house. He quickly ducked behind his trailer, and for a second, he thought that Jacob had seen where he went, but all three boys stopped in front of his house.

They stood on the sidewalk, fuming, talking about what they were gonna do to him. To *HIM. Jesse!* How'd they know it was him? It didn't really matter. It wasn't an important part of the plan.

Right on time, there came a timid voice, "Hey."

Jacob and his friends turned toward the voice and saw another ninja.

The other ninja stood in the dark on the sidewalk in front of Owen's house. "Looking for somebody?" he said. With that, the ninja removed his mask and revealed himself.

Jesse's mouth dropped. *That* definitely wasn't part of the plan.

The older, much larger boys started walking toward Owen, who stood his ground.

Jacob walked right up to Owen. "Well well," Jacob said, "if it isn't the friendly neighborhood book nerd." Curtis and Tommy snickered from where they stood, behind Jacob.

"Whatcha doin', book nerd?" Jacob asked, looking around, "And where's that nerd of a brother of mine? Or are you two not friends anymore? Can't say I blame ya though. I wouldn't wanna be friends with someone that would just stand there and watch me get beat up." Again, laughter from Curtis and Tommy.

From the darkness behind Owen's house walked Jesse, mask removed as well. He stepped to Owen's side. "That's a mistake I won't do again," Jesse said, giving Owen a pat on the back.

Suddenly, Jesse heard something he never thought he'd hear. "Why don't you jerk-holes just get to steppin'." The words had come from Owen and Jesse was just as surprised to hear them as the older boys were.

Jacob actually took a step back. He paused a beat but then composed himself and stepped back up and gave Owen a push. "Why don't you make us."

With that, Jesse stepped forward and pushed his brother away from Owen.

Jacob didn't fall down but he stumbled...and that was enough. He was furious now. He rushed forward and bumped his chest into his brother.

Jesse fell to the ground but immediately popped back up and rushed toward Jacob, who just stood there, unafraid.

The two brothers stood glaring at each other until Curtis stepped up from behind Jacob and whispered something in his ear. Jacob then looked down at the bag lying on the ground next to the neighbors yellow Monte Carlo.

His excitement rose when he saw the bottle rockets and a roman candle sticking out of the top of the bag.

He nodded at the bag, "Those yours?" he asked.

Owen, stepping forward, put a gentle hand on Jesse's chest to back him off. "They're mine," Owen said.

Jacob looked back at Owen. "Okay so here's how it's gonna go. I'm gonna forget about all...this." He motioned to Jesse. "We're gonna take the bag and go back to doing what non-nerds do."

Jesse rushed forward again, "Heck no, those are ours!" he said, "We bought them ourselves." Owen, once again, gently pushed his friend back.

"Go ahead," Owen said diplomatically. "Take them."

Curtis and Tommy started laughing again. Jacob turned and smiled at them over his shoulder as Curtis stepped off the sidewalk to retrieve the bag of fireworks.

As he was reaching for it, Jacob suddenly said, "Wait." Curtis froze, just before grabbing the bag.

Jacob had a quizzical look on his face. His gaze shifted to Jesse but he spoke to Curtis, "Hang on a sec."

"You must think I'm stupid," Jacob said, this time speaking to Jesse. "I'm not sure what you're up to, but this doesn't feel right."

He walked over and knelt down next to the bag. Curtis, not sure what was going on, quickly backed away. Jacob used a single finger and flicked the top of the bag open. He gazed inside, not sure what he was looking for.

Jacob looked up and motioned for Owen to come over. "You open it." he said. Owen did as instructed, holding the plastic grocery bag by the handles. He held it open for Jacob to look inside.

Once Jacob was satisfied that the bag was clear of any suspicious objects, he said to Owen, "Now pick it up." Owen, once again, did as instructed. Still holding just the handles he held the bag out to Jacob, who took it slowly but didn't move otherwise.

Everyone froze. The moment seemed to last forever until Jesse stepped forward, "Are we good then?" he asked, impatiently.

Jacob waited another few seconds, staring at his brother, then closed the bag. "Yeah, we're good." He said finally, "Now get outta here."

Owen and Jesse began walking away, slowly at first. They began to pick up speed as Jacob, still holding the bag, turned toward his friends.

Jesse and his friend were speed walking when Jacob began to feel the stickiness of the bag in his hands. In the darkness, it was impossible to see what was on the bag, but it made his hands sticky as well.

He had taken just two steps when he felt the tug on the bottom of the bag. The rest seemed to happen in a flash.

The tug on the bag had come from the fishing line that stretched all the way back to the top of Tom's nice, clean car. The line was attached to a small piece of wood that was holding up another, larger piece of wood that held three paint cans.

The fishing line pulled the first piece of wood out from under the larger piece and all three cans of paint went tumbling down the front windshield of the car, spilling paint the whole way.

White paint splashed down the windshield and the hood of the car, making a huge mess and an even bigger racket.

Jesse and Owen had paused, only slightly, to witness their moment of triumph and were not disappointed. It went even better than they'd planned.

The older boys had been just a few steps away from the car when the paint spilled so as the cans rolled down the hood, paint splattered all over the ground and all over them.

They tried diving out of the way but it hadn't helped. All three of them had been splattered with white paint.

Owen and Jesse started moving again. They had no intention on being around when Jacob put the pieces together.

They were rounding the corner to Jesse's house when something unexpected happened. Owen's porch light came on. Jesse knew all along that Tom would see the mess on his car and eventually find out that Jacob had done it but his catching the boys in the act was better than he could have hoped for.

Tom came out onto the porch just in time to see the boys getting to their feet, covered in paint. "What the…?" Then he saw the paint cans on the hood of his car and absolutely blew up!

"You little punks!" he screamed as he practically dove off of the porch at the boys.

The last thing Jesse saw before Owen pulled him away was Jacob holding his hands up and trying to explain what had happened to Tom.

Jesse gave Owen a lift into his bedroom window and then Owen helped pull him up. They quickly changed back into their other clothes and hid all of the black ninja stuff in the closet. Then they sat down and started playing *Bug Annihilator* on the small TV that Jesse had in his room.

They could hear some of what was going on outside, but it was two lots away so they just sat and played the game.

Suddenly, there was a loud banging on the front door and shortly after that, they could hear Tom yelling.

The boys left the bedroom, acting curious about what was going on. They saw Tom standing just inside the door, "Your punk kid ruined my paint job!" he was saying.

Jesse's mom was trying her best to calm him down. "Okay, okay, okay…listen," she pleaded, "he will clean it up. I don't care how long it takes but he will fix it."

Just then, Jacob walked in the house. Tom turned to him, and if Jesse's mom hadn't been between them, Tom may have hauled off and punched Jacob. Luckily, that didn't happen.

"To your room," his mother said to Jacob, sounding furious, "NOW!"

Jacob stood there with paint splatters all over his face and down the front of him, "But mom. It wasn't me," he said, and then caught sight of Jesse and Owen. "It was them!" he screamed, pointing at the younger boys, who stood there acting confused.

"It couldn't have been them," she said, still sounding furious, "They were here all night." She grabbed his hand, "Look, your hands are covered in paint too, and this isn't the paint splatters."

With that, they went back into Jesse's room and closed the door. They sat back down and started playing the game again. Neither one spoke for a long while. Then Owen let out a snicker that he just couldn't hold in any longer.

Hearing his friend laugh made Jesse snort. He actually snorted from trying to hold his laughter in. Now they were both laughing hysterically, though they managed to keep it low enough so no one outside the room could hear.

Through their laughter, they managed to give each other a high five because they knew that the plan had worked. They weren't sure what tomorrow held for them but for once, they didn't care. They knew that their friendship could hold up to whatever the future held so tonight was just about enjoying their victory.

Chapter Ten

The next day came. Owen woke up first. He opened his eyes and saw Jesse, still asleep, facing him. His mouth was agape and drool was spilling out onto the pillow. He snored lightly.

Owen reached over and lightly pinched Jesse's nose. After a few seconds, Jesse started to snore again but found he couldn't. He jumped up, suddenly awake but confused. "Wha…?"

Owen laughed harder than he could ever remember laughing. "What the heck, dude?" Jesse said loudly. That made Owen laugh even louder.

Finally, Jesse laughed too, though not as loud as Owen.

Later that day, Jesse was in his front yard, trying to keep out of Jacob's way but secretly enjoying watching him clean the front of Tom's car while Tom sat in a lawn chair and watched him.

Owen came walking down to Jesse's house carrying something.

He walked up to Jesse and sat down in the grass next to him. He handed over the object he'd brought over. It was a book. "Here dude," he said. "For you." He didn't really look at Jesse. He was transfixed on Jacob washing the car.

"*The Harrowing Adventures of Colton Tripp - Volume Two*," Jesse read the title of the book aloud.

Owen looked at him and smiled. "I thought you'd like it. After all, we've got a long summer ahead of us, and we're gonna need some more adventures."

Jesse returned his friend's smile. "Thanks, book nerd."

Owen laughed. "You're welcome, book nerd." Then they both laughed and went back to watching Jacob clean the car.

After a while, another car pulled slowly onto their street. It was an old minivan. It pulled into a slot on the opposite side of the street in front of a trailer a few down from them.

A man exited from the driver's side. He stretched his arms above his head and waited for the woman who had gotten out of the passenger side.

The woman walked around the front of the car and embraced the man. Together, they began walked up to the trailer. Then the woman stopped, looked back and said, "You coming?'

With that, the rear door of the car opened and a kid got out. He wore jeans with a red T-shirt and had a baseball hat on. He reached into the back seat and pulled out a box. He closed the door with his hip and began following the couple.

Jesse stood up and took a few steps toward the kid. "Hey kid," he yelled. The kid stopped and looked around.

"Hey, you moving in?"

The kid saw Jesse and nodded. "Yeah," he said.

Owen stood up and went to stand with Jesse. Together, they walked toward the kid. "What's your name, dude?" Owen asked, as they walked.

The kid put the box down on the lawn and turned to them and said, "Sam."

Jesse said, "I'm Jesse. That's Owen," and jerked a thumb at his friend.

The kid smiled and said, "Nice to meet ya." With that he reached up and took the hat off. Long blonde hair fell to his...*HER* shoulders.

Both Jesse and Owen's mouths dropped open, and they just stood and stared wide eyed at her. Then they looked at each other.

Finally, they looked back at Sam and said in unison, "Never mind."

They turned as one and walked away without another word.